Zachary
A Seagoing Cowboy

Shirley Miller Kamada

Black Rose Writing | Texas

This is a work of fiction. Names, characters, businesses, places, events, and incidents are either the products of the author's imagination or used in a fictitious manner. Any resemblance to actual persons, living or dead, or actual events is purely coincidental.

ISBN: 978-1-68513-640-6
LIBRARY OF CONGRESS CONTROL NUMBER: 2025932542
PUBLISHED BY BLACK ROSE WRITING
www.blackrosewriting.com

Printed in the United States of America
Suggested Retail Price (SRP) $16.95

Zachary: A Seagoing Cowboy is printed in Garamond Premier Pro

*As a planet-friendly publisher, Black Rose Writing does its best to eliminate unnecessary waste to reduce paper usage and energy costs, while never compromising the reading experience. As a result, the final word count vs. page count may not meet common expectations.

Praise for
Zachary: A Seagoing Cowboy

"This sequel to No Quiet Water gently addresses for young readers the injustices of war. Transporting us this time to Japan, Zachary's goodwill mission brings him face to face with the emotional and physical realities of the aftermath of war."
–**Peggy Reiff Miller, Heifer Project historian and author of** *The Seagoing Cowboy*

"A powerful coming-of-age tale about a young Quaker boy who sails across the Pacific bringing hope to postwar Japan—but ultimately confronts both the scars of war and the prejudice still lingering not just at home, but on the ocean between the two countries."
–**Cam Torrens, bestselling author of the** *Tyler Zahn mystery series*

"Hopeful, heartening, yet searing, Zachary: A Seagoing Cowboy is a gentle poem of a book, illuminating aspects of an era we may think we know well. As she did in No Quiet Water, author Shirley Miller Kamada reminds us the cost of World War II was born not just by the soldiers on the field, but by the civilians caught in the conflagration."
–**Pamela Norsworthy, author of** *War Bonds* **and** *The Florentine Entanglement*

"While we are dropped into Ms. Miller Kamada's novel in a gentle manner that belies the drama to be revealed in its final pages, the beginning is fitting to deepen the impact of the young man's revelations upon arriving in Japan a few years after WWII. The author's research is clear from page one, providing the reader with a compelling experience that tracks with Zachary's. The understated literary style suits the narrative, stripped of unnecessary emotional descriptions, stark at times in the extreme..."
–**Samantha St. Claire, author of** *The Case of the Peculiar Inheritance* **and** *Comes the Winter*

*With love, for my husband, Jimmy Fumio Kamada,
who came into this world a prisoner of his own government—
his parents' crime, the color of their skin.*

Zachary

A Seagoing Cowboy

Peace is a verb.
—Unknown

So let us try what love can do.
—William Penn

CHAPTER ONE
Seagoing Cowboys

Here I am, eight hundred miles from home and about to be a whole lot farther. A few months ago, I was sitting on a sturdy branch in a big leaf maple tree, considering my math homework. Trigonometry.

In front of me now looms a massive white structure, pulsing, vibrating, thrumming, as though it were alive. The SS *Contest*, a C2 refrigerator freighter. Huge cranes rise over the hull. Identifiable by khaki-colored uniforms, caps, and insignia, merchant marines swarm the dock.

Wading into a restless mass of goats, avoiding their sharp, double-pointed hooves, I am shoved, jostled hip high by an onslaught of two hundred twenty-seven goats. One goat bumps me hard, at the back of my knee. The knee buckles, and I extend a hand to keep my balance. Soft muzzle, shining eyes. Scamp. She is laughing at me. Of these goats, all but forty are female, does bred specifically to deliver kids after we reach Yokohama.

A heavy, almost viscous odor slaps me in the face and clings, so bitter it briefly stops my breath. I'd been warned about bucks, their smell. And the racket they make!

The four men who are overdressed for herding goats must be Mr. Schmoe's volunteers. Seagoing Cowboys. They look frazzled. Others, youngsters, men, and women, many in coveralls, all wearing gloves and sturdy boots, appear experienced at wrangling and work together easily.

Donated from family farms, the goats, mostly white or cream-colored, have come to the ship in small trucks and in trailers behind pickup trucks, with men, women, and children wedged onto single-span seats. I know from experience someone is straddling the gearshift.

Then, "Zachary? Hey! I thought that had to be you!" A young man reaches his hand toward me. "I'm Lee. Lee Richards. Zachary Whitlock, right?"

I'd guess he's a little older than I am. His hair is covered by a lightweight knit cap. His eyes are framed by glasses, the kind that make him look intelligent. His hand is still out. I grasp it and shake. My face warms.

"I—"

"Nearly intolerable, isn't it?" Lee asks. "We keep goats at our place, but only fifty or so at a time. Wow. Loud."

At a tug on my sleeve, I look down. Not a goat. A little boy. Gray eyes, a cowlick.

"My mother said we would see cowboys. Where are your horses?"

A woman carrying a parcel with a blue and white cloth knotted over it, probably some necessity for traveling with children, pats his shoulder. I know from my friend Fumio that this cloth is called a furoshiki. His mother gave me a plate of cookies wrapped similarly before I left on this trip.

The boy turns. "Mama, I—"

"Teddy, I'm sure these men are too busy to visit with you right now."

"But you said! Cowboys!"

"Seagoing Cowboys, Teddy."

"But you're supposed to be cowboys." He frowns at me. "I wish you were a cowboy."

Right now, I do, too.

•   •   •

Something enormous throws a shadow over my shoulder. I turn, tilt back my head. From the ship rises a sort of elevated cabin, as on a ferry boat, but immense. Fronted by glass panels, like car windshields, except bigger. Much bigger.

"That's the bridge," a crew member says. He's young, but older than me. His uniform is crisply pressed, and his shoes are so shiny I can't help but notice.

"Sorry?"

"That." He points. "What might be thought of as a tower, on a ship it's called the bridge."

"Oh. Thanks."

The bridge. I'd never have come up with that. A bridge is longer than it is wide, sometimes iron, sometimes concrete, the ones near our house are wood. Those bridges go from someplace to someplace.

"You're a Seagoing Cowboy, right?"

Strange nickname, but, as Mr. Schmoe told me, in the Heifer Project's early days milk cows were donated to starving communities. The name fit better then than it does now, I guess. I force a grin.

"I've met a few of you Seagoing Cowboys. Most are more comfortable on land than at sea. You?" His expression tells me that wasn't a question. "Those goats you're taking to folks in Japan are real fine. Saanens! You're going to be one busy Cowboy. My name's Eddie Vasquez. I'll see you around."

With the animals settled in, and merchant marines readying the ship to get underway, the people who donated the goats approach Mr. Schmoe and the other Cowboys to shake hands. Mr. Schmoe speaks with each of them. In many cases, these goats are replacing, if such can be said of a living being, animals that were killed in the war's hostilities. Mr. Schmoe writes in a small notebook he carries in a pocket. Addresses, probably. I imagine he'll send a personal note.

I hear talk of shared blessings. I see tears on the faces of some goat owners. Grown men wipe their eyes. My own eyes sting. What of our flock of sheep at home? Would I be so selfless? Could I raise them and then let strangers take them to a devastated land so far away?

The clamor, the smell, the sounds of a cargo ship readying to set sail. Sharing farm animals, a livelihood, hope. I lean into it all.

• • •

Mid-morning on the SS *Contest*. A deep voice calls. "Fourth Engineer Vasquez!"

"Yes, Sir!" Eddie salutes.

"You seem to have plenty of time. Take this kid—*er,* this young man—and the other volunteers below. Show them where to put their gear. Mr. Schmoe is bunking in the officers' quarters." He looks toward me. "He asked me to tell you, you *Cowboys,* that he'll meet up with you in about an hour. So, Vasquez?"

"Yes, Sir! Right away, Sir!"

When the officer was out of earshot, Eddie spoke quietly, "Don't worry about that. Well, then again, do. He's the Chief Mate. But he's a good guy. Fair."

"There's Lee Richards." I wave. "Lee!"

In this commotion, he can't hear me, but then Eddie whistles, earsplitting, sharp.

My friend Fumio back home can whistle louder, however. He used to wait on his bicycle with his dog Flyer in front of my house when I was late getting ready for school. If I was too late, he whistled. My mother always said his whistle could bring a stone statue to life.

Once more Eddie whistles. Lee turns, lifts his hand, and alerts the others.

"Men," Eddie says, "let's walk. I'm going to give you a vocabulary lesson."

Walking. Easier said than done. Step left, ship leans right. Step right, ship goes left. We're not even out of the harbor yet. I try to give my attention to Eddie.

"Sailors, for instance, would not say we are walking on a floor." He scuffed his shoe lightly. "This is a deck."

That much I knew.

He leans toward a wall. "This is a bulkhead."

We reach a set of stairs. Steel, of course. Everything on a ship is steel.

"This is a ladder."

A ladder? I wonder what sailors call an ordinary, garden variety ladder?

"Down the hatch, now!" Eddie laughs. "On a ship, we never go downstairs, we lay below."

Dropping into a dim space below deck, I hear a man murmur, "Just call me Jonah."

Eddie continues, "And this is a passageway. Not a hallway. A passageway."

It turns out the four of us are sharing one compartment. We find our bunks, drop the bags of gear that we'll unpack later, and follow Eddie.

The two hundred twenty-seven goats are in pens constructed of prefabricated panels, lightweight metal held together with specially designed joints, some of which obviously have failed and have been replaced with twists of baling wire. The panels are arranged on the main deck, aft of the superstructure. Aft means the back, the last section of the ship as it sails into port. The superstructure is like a tall building reaching into the sky near the center of the ship. It houses the captain's base of operations. The bridge. I would love to get up there to see the equipment and how it's used.

The goats have quieted and are calm, by appearances. With so many, I may never fully be aware of what is happening with any one of them. How great it would be if Flyer were here to help keep them in line, the way he does with sheep. Flyer belongs with Fumio, though. Their family is busy farming soybeans. There's a good market for soybeans right now.

The ship has been supplied with provisions, bags of protein and mineral mixture for feed, bales of hay for browse and fiber, which helps the butterfat content in a mother goat's milk. I'm surprised to see that the metal feeders in the goats' pens are full, and that hay is in the mangers. Straw lies in bunches, for now, near the pens' corners. Mr. Schmoe says a few donors who had a hard time leaving their goats behind did all this.

Continuing, Eddie tells us the port side is the left side of the ship.

Lee asks, gesturing with his hand, "Left?" Then he turns a one-eighty and asks again,

"Left?"

Eddie shakes his head. "Left when you are looking toward the bow. The pointy end. The part of the ship usually moving forward. Right is starboard when you are facing the bow. The stern is the back."

I am seeing in real-life the meanings of terms I had only seen on paper before today. Back on the Island, I found a book about the shipping industry that included a glossary I copied out and have kept in my pocket:

- *Openings in the outside of the ship are ports, not windows.*
- *Entrances from one compartment to another are called doors.*
- *Openings from one deck to another are called hatches.*

- *The handles on the watertight hatch or door are called dogs.*
- *When you close a door or watertight hatch, you secure it. If you close down the dogs on the door or hatch, you dog it down.*
- *You never scrub the floor or wash the walls, rather, you swab the deck and scrub the bulkheads.*
- *When you get up to go to work, you turn to.*
- *You never go downstairs, you lay below, and if you are going <u>up</u> from one deck to another, you lay topside.*
- *If you are going up the mast or into the rigging, you are going aloft.*

"Especially because of the work you'll be doing," Eddie says, "this term is interesting. The location where pails and pitchforks, rakes, shovels and the like are stored is spelled as if it was *'tween-decks*. Sailors say 'twin-dex.' It means between decks."

•   •   •

Two of our fellow Seagoing Cowboys started looking kind of green this afternoon and had to go to the cabin. Only Mr. Schmoe, Lee, and I feel well enough to supply the goats with fresh water, minerals, and feed.

Hay is kept out of the weather below the main deck, in the ship's hold. Bales must be raised by block and tackle, twice every day. Many hands are needed, below and up top, to work the winch and control the load's swing. I'll study that piece of equipment later, try to see it as a mathematician would, or an engineer.

The SS *Contest* is a machine. A floating, rolling, bucking machine. Beyond massive. Systems controlling systems. Organized to the nth degree. The "n" stands for noisy. This ship is never quiet.

Before bedtime last night, I felt as if my head were floating far above my body, my vision blurred by a gray veil. I asked a clerk if I could borrow a wastebasket. As off-kilter as I felt, I noticed his red hair and drift of freckles. A kindred spirit.

He grinned. "A landlubber. Seasick, no doubt. Hey, before bringing it back would ya—"

I nodded hard once. *Yes*. And bolted. Made it to the passageway just in time. Then took the wastebasket to the head to rinse it.

Back in the cabin, sounds of retching punctuated the darkness.

The next eighteen hours felt endless. Nausea, dizziness, uncontrollable vomiting, and disorientation. Where was I? How did I get here?

•   •   •

"Whitlock!"

"Yes, Sir."

"When you've scooped the . . . manure, speak with Fourth Engineer Vasquez."

"Yes, Sir. Right away, Sir."

This is going to be awkward. The manure is on my shoes. Its odor must be in my clothes, my hair. The smell will be hard to lose.

For the past few days, every time I've seen Eddie Vasquez, he was bringing a Seagoing Cowboy—sometimes me—a basin. Something to throw up in. The uncontrollable spewing. The bitter taste. The sour smell. It's been awful. Eddie has never so much as made a face. There are medics. They look in on us, too. But Eddie seems to understand the feeling of being unmoored and steps up, even though it isn't his job. When the worst of the seasickness passed and I could think clearly, I thanked him and said, "I'm pretty sure this isn't your job, Eddie."

He told me his duties were concerned with the ship's main propulsion systems, water systems, air compressors, and the sewage treatment plant. *Yes, sewage*, as well as many other systems. "I am involved in the ship's bunkering operation. That's refueling. Sometimes the ship goes *to* the fuel, in a harbor. Sometimes a barge brings the fuel alongside."

"Wow, that sounds *very important!*" I couldn't think of a better way to express my awe.

"It is, Zachary. I've passed the required exams and training courses, basic safety, part of that is firefighting, studied log keeping."

"Math?"

"You bet. Lots of math. Lots of work. Now, as Fourth Engineer, I'm part of the Engine Company's chain of command. On land, I'm from Arizona. My parents and brothers and sisters, we keep a large herd of goats. For milk, cheese."

Easy to see Eddie likes animals. I think he enjoys helping us out. Captain Townsend has good reason to accommodate that.

Strangely enough, from time to time I feel hungry. But my hunger is at odds with the certainty of vomiting.

CHAPTER TWO
The World at War

1942. I was eleven, and we were at war.

I sat at the edge of the pine forest holding a folded-over peanut butter and strawberry jam sandwich, technically half a sandwich. My stomach was in knots, as it had been since the war started. Flyer, my friend Fumio's border collie, sat beside me, his ears drooping. I tore off a piece of the sandwich, held it toward him. "Not hungry either?"

His weight pressed hard against me.

Below us, Bainbridge Island's Eagle Harbor and the Winslow shipyard buzzed with electricians, engineers, and steelworkers building minesweepers.

Big doings on a small island. Four radio antennas pierced the sky. A sub-snagging steel net blocked the Rich Passage waterway.

My best friend and next-door neighbor Fumio, Flyer's *person*, and Fumio's family—*Flyer's* family—the Miyotas, were forced to leave. All because the Japanese military had bombed the U.S. Pacific Fleet at Pearl Harbor the previous December. They had to leave their home, their crops and animals, and, as they were the second generation to work their land, their family's history. My parents, my brother Jacob, and I were caring for their property and ours as best we could. Everyone was working hard. Everyone was tense. Adults in our island community whispered and watched the sky. It was hard to pay attention in school. Homework didn't seem as important or as much fun as when I was doing it with Fumio. No one knew what the outcome was going to be. Planes buzzed overhead day and night. My parents listened through the static to news on the radio every evening. We heard words like Nazis. Hitler. The SS. Jews. Franco. Mussolini. Hirohito. Allied forces.

The day Fumio and his family were taken from the island was the worst day of my life, of Flyer's life, and I'm sure of Fumio's, too. They were forced to hang tags on their coats. They were allowed to pack only one suitcase each, so they wore as many layers as possible in order to take extra clothing. They were loaded onto a ferry like they were, well, like they were sheep, or cattle, and then they were gone. To a land of nothing but dust, dust, dust. The government had built barracks in the desert as housing. A place with no water and, as some said, no hope.

They stayed first at Camp Manzanar near the White Mountains in California, then travelled by train and bus to a lonesome outpost called Camp Minidoka in southern Idaho. We got letters from them with big ink marks crossing out certain words and sentences. My mother missed Mrs. Miyota, with whom she was always trading pies and jams and garden crops and recipes and pieces of fabric and advice for raising us children. My father missed Mr. Miyota, with whom he consulted and partnered on everything related to running farms and handling the business end of it. I missed Fumio every single day. And Flyer, who spent much of his time sitting on our porch and watching the road that passed in front of our houses, as if waiting for his family's return, clearly missed them, too.

CHAPTER THREE
Vulnerability

A ship's rattle and roar is rhythmic, the various elements, subtle. Goat noises are also rhythmic, and with this many of them, roar is a good word for the sound. Goats, though, are in no way subtle. They make all kinds of different noises, and most are loud. Some bleats are one long syllable, some multiples, some are in the upper register, ear-splitting, some a growl. What are they saying to each other? I have no idea, but I'm guessing nothing happy right now.

One cry rises above the rest, though. It is higher-pitched and disturbing. Off-key. Following the sound, I find a doe struggling, trapped in a section of temporary railing, fighting to free herself. Her leg is scratched, bleeding. I approach carefully. She needs help, but she's afraid, and those hooves are sharp.

Last night I went to bed fully dressed, too sick to do otherwise, so I'm still wearing my belt, which I remove, wrapping the doe's hind legs loosely, careful of the buckle. I must work quickly, though, or she'll injure herself further.

"Zachary?"

"Mr. Schmoe! Good morning, sir."

"Yes, it is a good morning! And Zachary, you needn't call me sir. Just Floyd, please. Could you use some assistance?"

"Yes, sir."

Mr. Schmoe chuckles. "Well, we can talk more about formal titles later. How can I help?"

"I need the halter. She's scared and in pain, but if I'm going to free her and treat this wound, I must be able to hold her, keep her still."

"Where will I find it?"

"In my animal care supplies kit, under my bunk. A dark green duffel. Could you bring it, please? This doe is injured."

"Yes, I see. I'll get it right away."

Floyd returns with my duffel, and I thank him.

"You good here?"

"Yessir. I can handle it."

"All right then. Send someone after me if you need a hand," Mr. Schmoe, Floyd, says as he leaves.

I can see this will not be a quick fix. The doe's leg is thrust through two pieces of twisted wire that secure the panels of a pen. Pulling it free risks making the scratch deeper. Although I'm handling her leg gently, she struggles. Leaning closer, I carefully circle her midsection, almost hugging her.

A sailor passing by pauses, stops. "Looks like you've got trouble."

Glancing up, I see dark hair, dark skin, tall.

He says, "I'm Vernon. You must be one of Eddie's new friends."

"Uhm, yes. I'm Zachary."

"Glad to meet you, Zachary. Anything I can do?"

"Wire cutters?"

"Sure. I'll be right back."

Once Amelia, as I've named her, is freed and the belt restraining her hind feet removed, I examine the leg. The cut is not as deep as I had feared. I coax her back into her pen, study the panels to assure they will hold. How did she get out, anyway? Of course, the pens were put up in a hurry. And pregnant animals are often apprehensive. Can be erratic. If this ship is strange to me, the young doe has good reason to be terrified.

I clean the cut, apply ointment, cover and tape the wound. I'll need to check it often. Infection might be fatal.

Vernon returns. I hand him the wire cutters. He nods to the doe and walks away.

Mr. Schmoe, Floyd, brings me scrambled eggs and toast, a spoonful of apple jelly on the plate's edge. A fork, a paper towel. I thank him and, surprised to be hungry, eat sitting on a bale of hay, wiping the last bite of toast across the remaining smear of jelly.

I run my thumb over Amelia's nose. "You okay now, girl? Don't be afraid. I'll be around. All day. Not going anywhere."

After turning in a circle, she settles into a bed of straw.

"Get some rest, Amelia." She will need it. Her sides ripple with the movement of her soon-to-be-born kids.

I take the surgical gloves to the head and clean them. Back in the cabin, I reorganize the animal care supplies and stow them. Finally, sitting on the edge of my bunk, I inhale deeply, close my eyes for a moment, and awake an hour later, slumped from my waist down on a woolen blanket, feeling as if I've become a pretzel. Straightening brings pain. My yelp draws attention.

"Zachary, you looked uncomfortable, but I didn't want to wake you."

"Thanks, Lee. But next time, please do."

From the unbroken vastness of the sea, I have come to a steel box with rows and layers of padded shelves, sleeping places for people I do not know. Bunks for sailors, one of whom is me.

I feel shut in by walls that aren't walls and the low structure overhead. I'm aware of every detail of the smell of people I've never considered before. Now I must accept that I smell, too. I am people. Like it or not, our odor goes with us, in fact, before us, wherever we go.

•　　•　　•

I learned that the term porthole refers to *part* of a portlight. A porthole, specifically, is the metal *frame*. When an opening is introduced in a structure, vulnerability is created. The installation of a porthole, the surround, strengthens the ship around the breach in the wall. The hinged glass cover is called a portlight. An open portlight can let in fresh air and light. It allows visibility. Open and unattended, it creates the possibility of a drenching. The word has run through my mind several times. Vulnerability.

I open the *portlight* and am hit in the face by the reek of fuel, like a gasoline engine going full bore. But this ship does not run on gasoline. It's the odor of diesel fuel that fills my nose, my mouth, and invades my eyes. Sneezing, I lurch backward, spewing spittle on the front of my shirt. Eyes closed, I feel for the portlight and close it.

This is bad. Something horrible is happening. My eyes burn. I find the door and hurry out into the passageway. Am I the only person who knows? If anyone lights a match, we're dead.

"Have a care, bud! You're on a ship, don't ya know?" I hear the chiding tone. "Ya can't sleepwalk to the head, hey?"

But I'm not going to stop. Disaster is moments away. I am bracing for the chaos I expect above, boots pounding, orders shouted, maybe a siren blasting.

What I hear is snoring. A cough or two. What I see is sleeping bags, duffels, and kits. Flashlights. Men might be reading, maybe writing letters home, or to sweethearts. Must be scores of men, snugged along bulkheads, out of the way of sailors on watch.

What I hear is goats, bleating, blaring. A herd of goats sounds distinctly different than a flock of sheep.

"Zachary!" Eddie calls. "I'm surprised to see you!" Eddie isn't panicking. He's in uniform, carrying a clipboard. "Is everything all right?"

"I . . . I opened a portlight. Diesel. The fumes." I'm embarrassed. My fear is unfounded.

"It's something, isn't it? New guys are always jolted the first time they experience it. It doesn't happen often, but if the wind is at our back and moving faster than the ship, a vacuum is created. Engine fumes are pulled into the air conditioning intake. You get used to it. Well, no, likely not. It's enough to knock you over. But not so bad when you know what it is."

"Thanks, Eddie."

Eddie goes back to his duties. I take in the sight of men who've left their bunks and are spending the night on the much cooler deck. I think of my nights sleeping in my brother Jacob's old Boy Scout tent, in the yard at our house. I wanted to know the feeling. To leave the four walls of my upstairs bedroom, throw down a bedroll and listen to the crickets. The herons, the owls. The howling of what few coyotes live on the island.

Here it's the same, but a different kind of same. The hum and loud moan of the engines, the clank of moving parts. The presence of sailors reading, sleeping, watching stars. The noise of water moves past us, uncaring as we glide through it, traversing it despite its lack of cooperation. It does what it does.

CHAPTER FOUR
Floyd Schmoe and the Big Leaf Maple

Early spring, 1948. An American Friends Service Committee meeting was in progress in our house. Several items of business were being discussed by a team of five members, who sometimes arrived with their children and occasionally a dachshund named Parker.

I sat in our big leaf maple tree, properly termed *genus acer macrophyllum*, which my older brother Jacob once said was planted as a memorial, although for what or whom, I don't know. With my back against its trunk, and my feet wedged into the crooks of its limbs, I'd long felt I was a part of that tree. Behind my ear a pencil, on my lap a clipboard and my trigonometry assignment. I could work on assignments and keep an eye on the lambs out in the pasture.

Trigonometry is the key to any number of pursuits. Medicine. Engineering. Agricultural science. It was offered at Bainbridge High during the senior year, but I wanted to challenge it. I had enough credits to graduate early, except for a math course, and math was my strong suit.

High school. I felt like I was just marking time, and I wanted to be finished with it.

Then what? I had a part-time job with the island's newspaper, first as a paper boy. (Of course, not all paper boys are boys. When we were eighth graders, my friend Reyna had a paper route.) Later, I took over what my employers called "the high school beat" and Young Farmers news. But I was nearly seventeen, and I wanted more. Maybe university? Maybe travel? I wanted to expand my horizons, as the phrase goes.

So, I went to the bank, took money from my account, purchased a money order, and mailed it to the American School of Chicago, Illinois. Fully accredited. Trigonometry was tough. And I liked that. It was fun.

From the pasture I heard a quiet mewling. A tiny woolly being, born early and wobble-legged still, was getting some sun and fresh air and an introduction to the big, wide world. I knew the lamb was fine for a while longer. I could continue working and return the lambs to the loafing shed a bit later.

Twigs snapped, footsteps through the grass.

"Hello."

Standing below was a friend of my parents, Mr. Floyd Schmoe. A Quaker. A conscientious objector. Almost a legend.

My brother Jacob was, too. Not a legend, but a conscientious objector. Because he would not carry a gun, some people called him a *conchie* during the war. That's rude.

Mr. Floyd Schmoe would not fight against the Central Powers in World War I. Violence all around. He would not kill. In Europe he worked with the Red Cross. Later, in Poland, he helped refugees find shelter, food, medical supplies.

He also worked for the Park Service at Mount Rainier as a naturalist and taught at the university in Seattle. Same as my parents, he and Mrs. Schmoe are American Friends Service Committee Observers. For the cause of fairness. Justice. They make it their business to visit places where people are being harmed for no fault of their own, but out of envy, prejudice, or greed, and they write about it.

"Room up there for one more?" Mr. Schmoe reached for a nearby branch. Long and lean, he levered himself up. "I'm interrupting you."

"It's okay. I'm stuck." I tapped the clipboard with my pencil.

"You'll figure it out. I asked after you, whether you were off to college. Your mother said it would be a while. You're a bit young still, she said."

"These are my trig calculations. I'm studying trigonometry by correspondence, through American Schools."

"American Schools? I've heard of that. Illinois, right? Trigonometry is usually taught in the senior year, isn't it?"

"Yes, sir. But graduation? I want to get a jump on it. I feel ready to be done."

"What courses do you still need, in order to do that?"

"Just this—trigonometry."

"I see! Well, your mother sent me, said I'd probably find you here, and she's about to serve crumb cake."

Lambs called from the pasture.

"Nice flock."

"Thank you, sir. They're Lincolns."

He braced to swing down. "I'll be heading inside."

"You can go back in through the window if you like."

He grinned. "Thanks, that's okay. I'll tell your mother you'll be in soon."

Leaving my clipboard in the tree, I got the lambs, bleating all the way, into the loafing shed. After climbing back up to retrieve my clipboard, I went in through the window and put away my math lesson. A sweet smell drifted through the hall door. Crumb cake.

One good thing about hosting a Friends Service Committee meeting is the food. Salads and desserts. Easy to pack in a car, handy to eat from a plate on the arm of a chair. Or on a lap. Mother has always kept linen napkins edged in her hand-crocheted lace for those occasions. No one expected me to sit through meetings, but sometimes it was interesting.

Pausing on the top step, I brushed grass and bits of leaves off my pantlegs, then retied a shoe lace. Mr. Schmoe's voice carried up the stairs. He was telling committee members about a project, delivering donated farm animals to families in Japan who had lost their homes and livelihoods because of the war. I heard, "Bombs. Innocent victims of conflict. Hundreds of thousands on the edge of starvation." I heard, "Goats. Cargo ship. Japan."

One of the Peace Churches was organizing voyages and supervising volunteers to care for the animals. Finding volunteers—he called them Cowboys, and friendly laughter followed—was not easy. Goats aren't as familiar as horses and cows, the more typical farm animals. No way around it, caring for livestock is hard work.

The conversation quieted then, and I wasn't much interested in less exciting news.

As I sat there on the stairs, the seed was planted. It sprouted and grew like bindweed. I could not get it out of my head. Mr. Floyd Schmoe was going to Japan. By ship. With goats.

For Mr. Schmoe, this was a way to aid suffering people and, also, to be permitted to visit Japan, since the country was under occupation by the Allied Forces and closed to all but a few civilians. After getting the goats to their destinations, Mr. Schmoe planned to talk with people whose advice he needed to get started on a project he felt passionate about. Building houses for those made homeless when the atomic bomb was dropped on Hiroshima.

A feeling rushed through me. Shaken to my bones. The voyage, the animal care, helping families in need. I wanted to be part of that. All of it

As a member of the Young Farmers Club, I'd helped transport sheep to livestock judging competitions. YFC members worked together to pen and care for the sheep, sometimes for three days duration. Goats couldn't be much different than sheep. I was sixteen going on seventeen. A couple hundred goats on a cargo ship to Japan? What could go wrong?

This was important, and I could do it. I knew I could.

But how?

Downstairs, I enjoyed the cake and hot chocolate Mother had made for the younger guests and me. Later, I helped straighten the front room, as always, and on the floor, under the end table beside the couch, I found a pamphlet describing the Heifer Project. On the front was a drawing of cattle walking up a ramp onto a ship. A cargo ship, I thought. Tucked inside the pamphlet were several pages of questions and instructions. An application!

Breathless, I found my favorite pen and went to my writing table. The questions seemed straight forward and reasonable. In answer to, "Do you possess any special skills that would be of value to the project," I wrote, "I have cared for our family's flock of sheep, which are ruminants, as are goats, since I could walk."

Giving "General Delivery," as my return address, I signed and dated the application, slipped the pages into an envelope, licked the flap, and ran my thumb, twice, along the closing.

On Monday, when the school day was done, I took the application to the post office, bought and applied a stamp, and dropped the envelope into the slot. Just before I walked out the door, the postmaster called, "Hello, young Mr. Whitlock. Say hello to your folks for me." I turned, lifted my hand and nodded, then went out to my bicycle. My stomach felt strange for a moment, but I pedaled toward home, and that feeling passed.

• • •

By evening, second thoughts came to roost in my mind. Why hadn't I told my parents what I was doing? Because I thought they might try to talk me out of a trip to Japan on a cargo ship? Or give me an absolute *no*? I was not, after all, eighteen yet, and they could forbid it. I was very responsible, though. So, I asked myself, if I was so responsible, why didn't I just tell them I'd mailed the application?

To be honest, I didn't want to tell my parents until I was certain I had a place on the Seagoing Cowboys team. I wanted notification of my acceptance. What if I didn't meet the qualifications, wasn't good enough? That would be humiliating. So, I waited.

But time did not. Calendar pages were turned, field work called for all able hands, and soon school would be let out. Eventually, though, I decided I had waited long enough.

• • •

Friday morning, I was last to get downstairs for breakfast. "Good morning. Sorry to be late." I laid the Heifer Project pamphlet on the table.

My father picked it up, studied the front, opened it. "Where did this come from?"

"Straightening the living room after the Observers meeting, I found it by the couch, under the side table."

"Oh." He cleared his throat. "You know, my friend Michael Walters was interested in this. Remember him, Doris? He was surprised to learn that to work on a freighter, even as a volunteer, he would have to join the Coast Guard and take an oath, even though a somewhat different form of the oath. He did not expect that."

I didn't expect that either. "How did your friend deal with it?"

"He didn't go."

"He didn't? Why?"

"I haven't seen him, so I haven't talked to him about that. But, I suppose, because—the Coast Guard! Military force. Guns. Referring to another person as *sir* and saluting."

What my father did not say, but what I knew, was that Quakers do not join the Coast Guard, nor any branch of military service, or law enforcement. No guns. No violence of any kind.

I couldn't sleep that night. I tossed. I turned. I paced. I went to the window, thinking of opening it, climbing through, and going out into the maple to think and look at the stars. But we were fogged in. Anyway, I shouldn't go out into the tree in my pajamas, and it wouldn't be safe to do that in my plaid flannel robe.

• • •

When I was ten, I didn't want to be a Quaker. Sitting in the maple, I thought about it often. Sometimes I laid my worries on Fumio.

He thought it was funny. "No one's going to make you be a Quaker, Zachary."

I never told Fumio, but my name is in the Book. Born into a Friends Society family, your name goes into a Registry. I also didn't tell him that it went back to the days of the British Empire when Friends were singled out as "non-conforming," because they did not follow the King's religion. Their names were listed. They were persecuted. That's history. Hard not to think of it in terms of the list Fumio was once on, Japanese Americans living along the U.S. coast. Quakers, though, put their own imprint on it. They made the list a point of pride. My name, Zachary Emerson Whitlock, is on a list. The Registry.

Maybe I grew up a little. Because eventually I recognized that in the long run, it's not so bad being part of a thing you believe in, a gathering of people who care about others and care about the world we live in and, out of respect for that, are willing to work to preserve what they value: dignity, fairness, peace for everybody. But walk away? I still felt like I could. Any time. It's a day-by-day kind of thing. Delivering goats is a peaceful undertaking. By joining Floyd Schmoe's effort, wouldn't I be putting my money where my mouth is, so to speak?

Leaning my forehead against the glass, through the darkness I heard a call. A great horned owl. I pictured it in my mind. An owl is vigilant, watching for the moment to descend, then pounces, gaining a meal. I decided right then to complete the Coast Guard application. In a way, I was putting it up to chance. Or fate. Perhaps once I'd made the effort to apply, my parents might look at things objectively and give their blessing.

In the meantime, there was much to do before I'd even be considered for the Project, and I planned to keep it secret. I wasn't lying to my parents. Just not telling the whole truth.

I'd have liked to talk to Fumio about it, the Coast Guard, but he was busy with field work in the soybeans. I think I felt guilty. I was contemplating a trip to *Japan*! He was Japanese American, and he'd never even been to Japan. No one in his immediate family had.

For now, I would keep my own counsel, and while I waited, evaluate my feelings about the Coast Guard. About everything. If my application was accepted, I'd receive a letter or a telephone call. I'd have to get to San Francisco on my own dime. If my application was accepted, I would decide *then*.

If my application was accepted? Despite my newfound, not-so-comfortable knowledge, I felt I already was a Seagoing Cowboy.

Did I have time to learn basic Japanese?

•　•　•

When I was seven years old, I wanted to surprise my mother with a birthday gift. Gloves, soft blue, velvet, with silver buttons. To wear to Society of Friends Meetings. I saw the gloves in a catalog. They would go with her sky-blue coat.

I'd have to send a money order. I had money in a piggy bank. Not enough for the gloves. But I thought how happy my mother would be, unwrapping the package, trying them on.

I thought maybe I could sell something to the owner of the thrift shop on the edge of town. Maybe my toy truck that I'd bought with my birthday money the year before.

Finally, I asked my father. He suggested I might work to earn the money.

What would I do? I had shoveled snow, once. Heavy work, and Jacob helped. But it wasn't snowing and, anyway, I wasn't paid for doing chores. Why would I expect to be paid for doing something my family needed done?

"Let me think," Father said, and after a moment, "Washing the truck is usually my job." Looking back, I remember he had named that truck Moby. If, he said, I washed Moby this time, he would pay me two dollars.

I weighed probably fifty-five pounds and stood four foot nothing. The truck was big. Father worked alongside me. The job would have been easier to do by himself, but he whistled while he used the chamois. He showed me how to use it, too.

I met the mailman Monday through Saturday for two weeks. When he asked, I told him about the gift for Mother. One day he brought a paper sack folded over at the top. "You can see what's inside by the words on the package," he said quietly. I hurried it to my room and tucked it under a too-big sweater in the bottom drawer of my dresser.

The day before Mother's birthday, while she was delivering handspun yarn to a customer, Jacob showed me how to measure wrapping paper and make neat corners. With one finger he held the ribbon in place while I secured the first knot. After a few tries, I tied the bow myself.

On Mother's birthday, Father made pancakes. After breakfast we went to the front room. Mother selected the gift from me first.

"From Zachary? Oh, what a surprise!" She patted the couch. "Come sit by me!"

She gently pulled the ribbon. The bow unfurled. She wound the ribbon into a loose coil and laid it down beside her. I held my breath as she took the lid from the box, moved the tissue paper aside. I know the words to use now: Her face lit up.

"Zachary! These gloves are beautiful. They match my good coat!" She laid her hand on my shoulder. "Perfectly."

Mother slipped her hand into the left glove, smoothed each finger, and touched the silver buttons, gleaming in the light from a window. She pulled on the right glove, extended her hands, looked toward me, smiling. "Who would have thought I might receive such a wonderful gift? The wrapping, such a good job!"

"Zachary did it himself, Doris."

"Jacob helped me tie the bow."

"Just the first one. Zachary's a quick student."

Mother wore the gloves while she unwrapped a book of poetry, and a book of French cookery. When she received a fancy jar of mint jelly, she removed the gloves before she opened it and held it to her nose.

Every Sunday, Mother wore the gloves to Meeting. After being seated, she removed them before Silence, and left them in her purse until time to leave. When they began to show wear, she chose a place on her dressing table, where they laid beneath the handle of a silver-framed mirror. Before they might become damaged, she said. They remain there now.

Up until I found out about the Heifer Project, that was the closest I'd ever come to keeping a secret from my parents.

CHAPTER FIVE
The No-Horse Cowboy

I crave fresh air. Levering open the portlight, the smell is not what I expected, nor is it what I crave. Not mild. Not salty. Well, you can't smell salty, but you can taste it. At the beach you might open your mouth to let the smell land on your tongue. Here I'm not tempted to open my mouth. The air reeks like the solution we use to scrub down the sheep shed.

Backing away, closing the portlight, I am enveloped by an intense human smell. A miasma. I've read that word, and it fits. Our quarters are noxious and putrid. They smell of illness, sweat, unwashed clothing. I'm tired but motivated to wash and change into clean clothes.

In the passageway, I run into the clerk with red hair and freckles who let me borrow a wastebasket when I was miserable with seasickness. I ask him where I might wash some clothing,

"Laundry? Too bad, Cowboy. There's a schedule and it's not your turn. Laundry is done one division at a time, and your division doesn't exist, *hmm*? Lots of water out there." He gestured. "Hang it on a yardarm and it'll dry fast. Stiff with salt. But clean. Or cleaner."

He's joking. I'm too near spent to find it funny, but my situation is not his problem.

"Hey, Zachary! You are Zachary, right? I'm Jameson. True enough, it's not your turn. But you've tagged your items, so they won't end up on the wrong sailor, right? You must be feeling kind of—"

How long since I'd brushed my teeth? Washed my hair? "Kind of disgusted with myself."

"Sure enough. Check in with someone in the Ward Office."

At home we are lucky to have a washing machine on our enclosed side porch. A round metal tub, hoses in and out, a wringer attached on top. "Be careful, Zachary," Mother always says. "Feed sheets, not your fingers, through the rollers!" After shaking the sheets hard to release wrinkles, we pin them with wooden clothespins to a line stretched between two poles.

On the ship, I have just learned, the tubs are big, more like barrels, positioned sideways with the door at the end. Wringers not attached. That's a separate operation. I asked Lee if he wanted to merge our loads. We'll need to do laundry a few more times during this voyage.

In the same room as the laundry equipment, on racks overhead, are what sailors call "whaleboats," used in case of an abandon-ship situation. I hope we won't need those.

●   ●   ●

I didn't expect much from the food served in a "mess" on a freighter. But the first thing I notice after putting on clean clothes, regaining my sea legs, and leaving my quarters, is the scent of fresh-baked bread.

All the meals are good. It can't be easy to lift and carry huge pans full of hot meat, potatoes, spaghetti, or maybe tuna casserole. I suppose the mess crew gets used to the constant rocking of the ship, but when big waves hit? I'd like to meet these cooks. Their legs and arms must be like timbers.

We Cowboys are assigned to eat with the officers, but I am responsible for the health and safety of the goats. They don't follow schedules. Sometimes I'm not properly dressed to eat at the captain's table. The crew eats in shifts, though. I asked for and was given the okay to eat in the crew's mess when it's more practical. And snacks are always available in the galley.

Our charges, the goats, occupy the main deck. The does on both the port and starboard sides and the bucks and their smell kept to the stern.

My brother Jacob's wife, Jessica, who is a veterinarian, loaned me a book after I was approved for the trip, which I studied from cover to cover. When she and Jacob were over for supper one night, we talked about goat care. "When working with goats, keep track of the bucks," she said. "Keep your escape route in mind. Bucks are defined by their determination to be the boss. They are aggressive, and they are always angry. Bullheaded. That's the word. There's this, too: Goats do not eat tin cans." She laughed. "No, seriously, they don't."

But goats do need fresh water and to be fed twice a day. Like cows and sheep, goats are ruminants, meaning they have four-compartment stomachs, also meaning they swallow without chewing. *Down the hatch*. Food enters the first compartment, then the second. Digestion turns it into cud. The goat upchucks. The food returns to its mouth where it's chewed again. Et cetera.

One morning I reached a pen just as a sailor pitched a snuff tin—empty I suppose—into it. I hopped the railing, retrieved the container, turned, and stopped myself from throwing it back at him.

"What are you doing?" Upset? You bet.

"Didn't mean no harm! I just wanted to see the goat eat it! I didn't have a regular tin can."

"Goats don't eat cans! What would that do to a goat's mouth, its throat?"

The man's head went down. "Sorry. I didn't think. I just heard they did."

"Yes. I heard it, too. Heard it so often I almost believed it. Until I gave it some thought."

"Good thing you showed up. I'd feel real bad if I caused harm."

"Right. I can see that."

•   •   •

Because we were told space was limited, I left behind a few items of my lambing gear when I packed. I brought only the essentials. My head lamp and a trouble light, for broader illumination. Medical grade gloves, standard and shoulder length. Iodine tincture. A halter. A leg snare and a kid puller, which is technically a lamb puller, but its purpose is the same. I sure hope I don't need either of those.

At home, alongside my sister-in-law Jessica, I helped deliver our flock's lambs. Hard work, kneeling in dirt, on concrete, sometimes mud if the ewe wanted solitude and delivered outside the barn. If a lamb is stuck in the birthing canal, it's hard to pull the baby out, your arm in past your elbow, hoping you're not hurting the ewe too bad. Goats are . . . I'll find out.

All those does, expecting babies, their milk coming in. Because the ship has no way to pasteurize it, the captain can't allow "human consumption" of the milk. Only Eddie drinks all he can hold. I dipped my finger in a pail and tasted it. Different from what I'm used to, but not bad.

Before we left the States, several people asked, "Why goats? Aren't cows better producers?" True, cows might produce more milk. But goats are compact animals. They maintain a stronger constitution on simpler feed. They're less messy. Bottom line, Japan is a mountainous country. Goats are perfect for that kind of terrain.

I'm glad these goats are not meat animals, but only for milking and breeding. They will live out their lives doing what goats do. Eating, maybe foraging some. Breeding, raising kids. And, so I'm told, climbing fences and making trouble.

Bringing fresh water to the pens, bucket by bucket, is time-consuming, but an important part of our twice-daily routine. The goats are comfortable in my presence. If I reach out, some snuggle the crowns of their heads into my hand, as this one, bright eyes, spotted ears, does now.

Working on this ship is a challenge. Not just learning my way around the ship but learning to approach situations as part of a team. This is not a do-it-yourself operation. The ship is big. Massive compared to machines I've dealt with before. It takes a team to keep it sailing.

First, I had to get acquainted with the other Heifer Project volunteers, five of us all together, a smaller team than is usually the case, I'm told. Two of our volunteers have been ill almost the entire time so far.

I've also made the acquaintance of many merchant sailors, and several of them lend a hand with feeding. Vernon helps with the milking whenever he can.

•　•　•

A lull falls near suppertime. The sun is low. The water is calm. We find ourselves drawn together, hashing out our day. Although they could have seen us as nuisances, SS *Contest*'s merchant sailors have made us welcome and crew members who are off shift, sailors and volunteers, come together on deck as the sun goes down. No plan. It just happens casually. Seldom is it the same people. At least one sailor who hasn't joined us before will invariably sit down and pull maybe a pack of gum or some other small offering from his pocket to share.

This evening, Floyd sits comfortably on an empty feed pail turned upside down. Most of the fellows sit flat on the hard surface. A few settle onto folded jackets, although nobody is wearing one. They are curious about us Cowboys, especially about Floyd. Some facts have been spread, plus a little gossip. They know he's written and published books, pamphlets, articles and, for official records, papers highlighting unfairness toward our country's Japanese Americans. He's friendly, outgoing. Never met a stranger, as people say.

I've been on the run all day and am happy to sit, legs stretched out before me and listen. As I care for the goats, the energy required for each step taken is doubled by the need to accommodate the ship's movement. Up and down and side to side. All the while searching the eyes of pregnant does for signs of *whatever*. Carrying buckets and moving bales is a lot of work, and tonight, especially, I feel it in my bones.

Pregnant does are restless, the kids inside them stirring, repositioning long legs, sometimes kicking, more and more as they near birth. Some does react by crying out, some by seeking solitude. I wonder if people are like that, too. Right now, I would *almost* like solitude. Not silence. But quietude would do.

Eddie joins us carrying a still steaming mug of coffee. He folds himself down to sit cross-legged on the deck, spilling not a drop, and rests the mug on one spit-shined shoe. "Nice evening! I have raisins, enough to share." He opens a paper packet and slides it toward the middle of our gathering. "Have one. Have two!"

"Thank you, Eddie!" Floyd reaches out, takes a raisin.

Lee, whose blond hair is tussled, as if it didn't see a comb today, takes two raisins. "Thanks, Eddie!" He pops one in his mouth, chews with the look of *thinking* on his sunburnt face. Then, "Floyd, you've seen a lot of the country, right? My father told me you lectured about Mount Rainier."

Floyd grins. "I was born in Kansas and live in Seattle. I suppose I've seen a few places in between."

"Do you have a favorite place?"

"I've had many favorites. Some places I've lived working as a park ranger and naturalist. Others I've visited, speaking for the National Park Service. More recently, my travel has been for the American Friends Service Committee, as an Observer." He glances toward Eddie. "We visited and evaluated the so-called relocation centers, the internment camps, where Japanese Americans were detained. Observers look for injustice, hoping not to find it. But if harm is being done, we report the conditions."

"What about France, Floyd?" someone asks. "I've heard you were a hero."

"I was a stretcher bearer for the American Red Cross, but only for thirty hours. True, bullets flew non-stop, and I did not carry a firearm. But others were in danger for much longer than thirty hours. Most of my time in Europe was spent helping refugees after World War I, building prefabricated houses and remodeling army barracks for displaced families. My weapons of choice? A hammer and a pocketful of nails."

"So, you've never used a gun?"

Floyd looks up at something only he sees. "When I was ten, against my mother's wishes, my father allowed me the use of a rifle. A twenty-two. I hunted rabbits, squirrels. I lacked the skill to take a life, for which I am grateful. I did trap skunk, muskrat, and opossum though, along a stream. I am ashamed of that. A cruel sport."

A question has been on my mind for a long time. Shifting my position to get more comfortable, I ask, "Mr. Schmoe. Floyd. What is the meaning, the derivation, of your name?"

He chuckles. "People always wonder, but few take the time to ask." He glances toward me and smiles. "It's not a pretty name, is it? 'Sch,' is

Germanic. 'Moe' is Scandinavian. Probably from a much older language. Frisian. That bears study. There's Yiddish mixed in there, also."

"So, the name Schmoe, in one or more of those languages, means—"

"Just as it sounds, Schmoe is 'schmuck' in English, which translates to foolish, boring, stupid."

"Really?" Lee asks.

"Mrs. Schmoe says the name makes us approachable. With a name like Schmoe, the bar is low."

"Floyd," someone else asks, "where's the strangest place you've ever lived?"

"My family and I loved living on Flower Island, in the San Juans in Washington state, but probably the strangest place I ever lived was the Muskogee, Oklahoma, jail."

"Jail! What?" A chorus of voices. "Why?"

"I was seventeen. My folks were traveling by horse-drawn wagon from Muskogee to Miami, me riding alongside on a bike I'd saved my money to buy. Passing through Muskogee, my mother gave me five cents and sent me into town on an errand, to go to the post office and buy five post cards. She and my father went on ahead in the wagon. I was to meet them at the bridge four miles north.

"I found the post office easily and bought the post cards. It was the first time I'd ridden on paved streets. I explored for a time and enjoyed it too much, I guess. When I reached the bridge at dusk my parents were nowhere in sight. The bridge-tender hadn't seen them. I rode back to town, didn't find them there, and finally returned to the bridge. The tender gave me a can of pork and beans and let me sleep on the tollbooth floor. The next morning, no breakfast, no money, I rode back into Muskogee. No one had seen my parents. As darkness fell, desperate and hungry, I headed for the police station. I was fed and housed in an empty cell in the women's jail.

"Incoming detainees were rowdy that night. Fights broke out. I have no idea if that was typical. The dividers between cells did not go all the way up to the ceiling, voices were raucous, and I learned many words I've never had occasion to use. Finally, my parents contacted police in Miami, who got in touch with the Muskogee police, and they put me on a train to Miami."

"As in Florida?" I ask.

"As in Oklahoma." Everyone laughs, and Floyd says, "Another raisin, please?"

•   •   •

The smell of toasted bread lingers in the air. The sun is well up, and I am adding straw to the goats' pens.

"Children! Slow down please." Two youngsters race into view, followed by their mother. I met her earlier. The woman carrying the furoshiki.

A little boy dashes toward me calling, "You're the no-horse cowboy!"

"I am, and you are Teddy."

Beside Teddy stands a girl who appears to be a little older, smiling. "Goats. They're cute. Can I pet one?"

"ThisisCassieshesmysister." Teddy spreads his arms and turns in a circle, like a helicopter wearing shoes. His way of speaking matches his movements: All is a whirr.

"Hello, Cassie. I am glad to meet you. My name is Zachary."

"See? He's just a kid, like us!"

"No, Teddy, he is not. He's not old like Papa," Cassie glances at me, "but he's a grownup."

"Please excuse us, young man. Zachary, am I correct?"

"Yes, Ma'am. Konnichiwa, Mrs. Blake."

"Yow! Mama, Teddy pulled my hair!"

"No, I didn't! Her braid fell into my hand. Anyway, I didn't pull hard."

Quietly, but in reprimand, Mrs. Blake says, "Shizukani, children."

Then to me, "Gomennasai. I apologize."

I nod, slowly. "Kodomo. Still learning."

"They are excited to see their father. Since Pearl Harbor, we live near my parents in Chicago. Of course, Japan is under occupation. But we are able to visit."

I don't know what to say. Whatever the specifics, the situation must be hard for the family. My reply? Another nod.

"Mister, can we pet the goats?"

Mister. I bite down on a smile. "Teddy, Cassie, goats are cute. But they're not pets. Mother goats might be angry if you get too close to their babies. Bucks, the big ones, especially."

"Boy goats."

"That's right, Teddy. They can be dangerous. They believe it is their duty to fight."

"Like soldiers! My father is in the Army."

"Father is a chaplain, Teddy," Cassie objects. "He does not fight. Besides, bucks have horns, silly."

"Can we ever pet the goats? The babies?"

"Children, we must go." Mrs. Blake takes them by the hand.

As they walk away, I hear Teddy's voice. "Maybe when the goat papa is not around."

• • •

Approaching the captain's table for the evening meal, I wait until Floyd lifts his bowed head, then go to the empty chair next to him. I pause, saying, "Captain Townsend, Sir," and am acknowledged, at which I pull out the chair and spread a napkin on my lap. "Floyd"—I'm barely comfortable calling him that—"we have a doe near giving birth."

"That's surprising. How do you know?"

"Restlessness. The doe lies down, stands up, lies down. Paws the deck. Also, she's bagged up."

"Bagged up? Ah . . . *Uhm*, we should talk about this later." He glances toward others at the table.

"Sure. Yes. But you can see the little bodies moving in their birth sacs. Twins! As the kids move, the doe, Amelia, her sides flex."

Someone chokes. Someone chuckles. Someone clears his throat. Floyd gives me a look to indicate *enough*.

"Yes, sir. Sorry."

Too enthusiastic. I've been told it is annoying. I've tried to overcome it. My face is a furnace. But what could be more important? Birth!

Then an image comes to me from home. In the attic, in a cabinet, a gift-wrapped package on the top shelf. I have to force myself to breathe.

CHAPTER SIX
My Birthday is in July

Old things have a life of their own. Who made them, and of what? Have they been broken, repaired? Leather cases, what do they hold? Baskets, why were they saved for use when the contents are not particularly secure?

On that morning the attic was a gathering of friends. A shelf of my childhood books, the rails and headboard for my "junior" bed, a baseball mitt too small for my hand, a rocking chair.

The musty smell was not a surprise. March and April were damp. Rain fell most days, with little sunshine between showers to dry our roofs, clear the bog from our lawns, or lift our spirits. Winter. War. Hiroshima, Nagasaki, decimated.

On sunny, dry days, Mother opened the door on the downstairs landing and also a screened window in the attic. A breeze flowed through. Maybe I should have offered to do that for her today. But my mission was to bring down three pair of knitting needles.

The storage space felt uncrowded. Two and a half years earlier, this space had been packed, fully packed, every inch, with the Miyota's most important possessions. An oval-framed portrait of Mrs. Miyota's grandparents. Lengths of silk. A large plate, Imari porcelain, bearing the family crest. Too much of a risk to leave them in their own home while they were away, even with Jacob living there. The FBI could choose to return at any time.

After walking through the door, I turned hard left. The yarn Mother produced for retail sales was kept in a metal locker, closed tight against any hungry moth that might sneak into the house. Her most important mail order sales item was hand-carded, homespun yarn. From our flock of sheep. The cabinet beside the locker was closed with just a hasp, no lock. But only two sets of knitting needles sat on the lowest shelf alongside a pair of crochet hooks Mother used for making lap throws. The next higher shelf was empty. Lots of things were still hard to come by, even with the war over. Everyone said it would take time for production and shipping to catch up. One more shelf. I'd need the stepstool.

Top shelf. A bunched shape wrapped in white tissue. A bow, pink and blue, and tied to a white, silken ribbon, a silver rattle. For a baby.

My hands acted on their own, pulled the package toward me. I took it down, put it on a table, and lifted the front piece of the little card:

Doris,

I'm so happy for you! Will the wallpaper be pink or blue? May I help you put it up? I might be ahead of myself, but three months will go by so fast.

In the blink of an eye your precious babe will be in your arms. You and Robert will have a new little angel. Jacob will be a big brother.

Extra special. An April birthday.

My birthday is in July.

In a flash of recognition, it made sense. The big leaf maple, as Jacob had told me, was a memorial tree. My parents had borne three children, not two. What happened? It was never said. I'd never asked. Why would I? But Jacob must have known.

Not the truth. Not a lie. A word I'd noticed because it sounds like math: Equivocation.

Almost without realizing it, I became even more determined to go to Japan.

•　•　•

To gain a place on Floyd Schmoe's team at age seventeen, I needed my parents' signed permission to join the Coast Guard. I would face whatever argument came.

My chair scraped against the floor as I moved it back. My steps jerky, I took my plate and silverware to the counter beside the sink and returned to the table. With or without notification of acceptance. I couldn't wait any longer to let my parents know.

"Mother, Father, I want to go to Japan."

My father eased his coffee cup onto the saucer. "Japan? Well! Maybe in a year or two? During the break between spring and fall quarters at the University? We can talk about that."

I took a deep breath. "I want to go much sooner. On the ship with Floyd Schmoe as a Seagoing Cowboy."

A forkful of scrambled egg was halfway to Mother's mouth. She lowered it to her plate.

After a moment of silence, my father said, "Son, you do know that volunteers for the Heifer Project have to join the Coast Guard to work on the ship, even as a volunteer?"

"Yes, sir."

"Zachary, we must talk seriously about this."

I had prepared for this conversation. What was most important for my parents to understand? I wanted to go to Japan. I wanted to do meaningful work, bring a message of friendship, address hunger, and I wanted to do those things on a gigantic cargo ship crossing the Pacific Ocean. I had to show my parents I was smart enough, mature enough, to make this choice.

"I haven't seen many places off the Island. Except for a few weeks on the road. In a farm truck, driving to Hunt, Idaho, looking for Flyer. Then visiting with Fumio and his family. In an internment camp."

"But Zachary, you went to a Young Farmers stock judging competition in Tacoma. And you accompanied a display of your mother's specialty yarn to Olympia for that craft show."

"Father, I don't mean disrespect, but I think your exceptions prove my point."

"All right. But Japan. Tell me why."

"Why? Because a mission like this might never happen again. Because I hope this never needs to happen again. Because I want to help. I've *got* to help. The horror of what they've lived through. Some of those people, maybe it would have been easier to die. What they've lost!" I paused and took a deep breath. Both my parents looked straight at me, giving me their full attention. "Mother, Father, I want to read something to you."

I stood and pulled from my back pocket a piece of paper folded into fourths, sat down again, unfolded and flattened it, cleared my throat. "'The United States Coast Guard is our nation's primary maritime operating agency, saving life and property at sea, protecting the marine environment'—*uhm*—" I resisted clearing my throat, "'enforcing federal laws and treaties, preserving'"—this part was good—"'marine natural resources, and—'"

As I read the passages aloud, they sounded different than they had in my head. If I wanted to convince my parents that it was all right for a Quaker, a Friend, to join the Coast Guard, I had to do it with the truth. Not a partial truth. The whole truth.

"'Conducting military operations, enforcing or assisting in the enforcement of all applicable Federal laws.'" Those phrases were not so friendly.

"'A branch of the Armed Forces of the United States at all times.'" I lowered the paper.

"But is that so bad? Doesn't somebody have to enforce the law, have to deal with the bad guys? To *maintain* peace?" I pictured myself at the front of a ship, jacket zipped high under my chin, my cap pulled low.

Father looked toward Mother. They held each other's gaze for what seemed forever.

Then, Father said, "We won't forbid this, Son. You're too old, now, for us to forbid you to do something. Unless it's illegal. Or deadly."

"Are we sure this isn't? Deadly?" Mother asked.

"Mother, the war has been over for two and a half years, and this would be a cargo ship."

"We've read about the SS *Cynthia Olson,* a cargo ship sailing between Tacoma and Hawaii with a load of lumber for the Army. Just lumber! Sunk by a Japanese submarine."

"I do remember, but Mother, that lumber was for the Army."

"I have read that merchant ships are often armed, fitted with heavy artillery. That could draw fire. Do you know that the seas around Japan were heavily mined during the war, and many of those mines were never retrieved? War is waiting, always, beneath a breakable peace. Violence, prejudice, manipulation. War is never over. Zachary, I fear for you."

My father put his hand on her arm. "Your mother isn't wrong."

"Mother, Father, can we do good without risk?"

"A great deal of good can be done with very little risk right here on Bainbridge Island."

Mother went to a cabinet, took out a plate, placed on it three oatmeal cookies from the cookie jar, and brought it to the table.

My father took a quart of milk from the refrigerator and poured a glass for himself. He held up the bottle. "Anyone else?" No takers.

I remembered sharing a cookie with Fumio during lunch at school. He used to break it in two and hand part back to me. Fumio wasn't much for sweets. We both came out ahead.

I missed that, the familiar routines, the easy friendship. But I was ready to branch out, try my wings. Or to see if I had wings.

Father returned to the table.

A few moments of silence, then—

"Zachary, the Coast Guard?" my mother asked. "You would do that? Really?"

"Son, it wouldn't be just six weeks for a trip to Japan," my father said. "It's putting your name, your life on the line. In writing."

"But how is that different from the Registry, the book of names of the Religious Society of Friends? My name is written there, and I didn't write it."

"I did, Zachary. Your mother and I did. We did it with such joy."

I wonder. Joy? Really? Thinking of the package in the attic, I bit my tongue.

$$\bullet \quad \bullet \quad \bullet$$

Hyacinths and daffodils bloomed and faded in the beds around our home. The buds on Mother's roses showed color. Lambing season had been extra busy, but now I watched only for late babies. I'd finished my trigonometry course and had a certificate from American Schools. Father bought a frame for it, and it hung in my room. I wore my cap and gown and walked down the aisle in our school gymnasium, a year early because of the trigonometry course. Afterward, Fumio and I sat in the big leaf maple with Flyer waiting patiently for us at the base of the tree, me asking, "Can you believe it?" After which I spilled the beans to Fumio about my plan and my impending trip to join the Coast Guard. He didn't say much. In fact, he didn't say anything at all, other than, "I hope things work out the way you want them to."

A week later, I was riding in the passenger seat of our car, and my father was driving us into one of Kehloken's underdeck levels. He'd had plenty of practice navigating into the dim, rumbling, inner space of a ferry.

According to our habit, and instructions on a sign posted at the parking area entrance—*Leave nothing in the vehicle. Stop the engine. Lock all doors—* we each grabbed a jacket, as the breeze would be stiff. Father dropped the keys into his jacket pocket, and we exited the car. I closed the passenger door. He patted his pocket to be sure the keys were there, closed and locked the driver's side door. We made our way to the observation deck at the boat's front and found a place to lean against the railing.

I felt no need to talk. The cries of seagulls sounded especially mournful as we got underway. Were they commenting on the rudeness of humans and their machines, expecting them to quit the space the gulls had established for bobbing and diving and harvesting their meal? Or questioning: What's so important, really?

Or was it laughter?

The rhythm of the waves was usually soothing. But not today. Today I would join up. Go against my parents' wishes. Become a member of the U.S. military. Leaving the house, I watched my mother hold back tears. I was sure that right now she was sitting in the old family rocking chair, yarn in her lap, knitting needles in her hands, not knitting. My mother's special handkerchiefs, saved for weddings and funerals, were edged in crocheted lace. This morning, she had tucked one under her sleeve's hem. It would be damp.

We'd been on the water half an hour, watching the shoreline come closer, listening to conversations muffled by the sounds of water and wind, and the engine's constant drone. As we approached the dock, the ferry slowed, the engine lugging down. Father and I returned to the car. Between us, we'd said five words: "There it is," and "Smith Tower."

At the entrance to the base, a uniformed Guardsman noted our license plate number, then handed the clipboard through the car window. Father signed the form. The Guardsman waved us forward toward white-painted, single-story structures atop a green, closely clipped lawn. We found a parking space. The car engine stopped. The silence roared in my ears.

Would Father say, "Let's talk about this," or "You can still change your mind," or give me that "I am disappointed in you" stare? I'd seen it often when I was thirteen, an awkward age.

The soles of my shoes felt bonded to the floor mat. I realized I was holding my breath and exhaled. I don't know how long we sat there in the silence. A half hour? Forty-five minutes?

Long enough that my father finally cleared his throat and said, "Zachary, you are my son no matter what choices you make."

A battle had been raging in my heart and my mind for weeks, but in that instant I did not doubt what I had to do. The Coast Guard was *a branch of the military*. The oath I'd be expected to take, as a stock handler, would be different. Fake, in a way. But I couldn't fake the Coast Guard. There's no playing at it. Plus, an oath of sorts had already been signed for me, in the Registry, the book of names of the Religious Society of Friends. Even though I didn't make that choice, was that an oath I could break?

Any oath is a real oath. You're committing yourself. I knew joining or not joining the Coast Guard was my choice, and no matter what I chose, my family would support me.

"Father, seeing this, *feeling* this place, a military base, confirms for me that this is not who I am. The Coast Guard would define me as I do not wish to be defined. Being here, it's all made clear. 'Good intentions do not justify questionable means.'"

"William Penn."

"Yes."

"And next he wrote, 'Let us try what love can do.'"

That quickly, I was done with indecision. In or out of the Society of Friends, I recognized that I, Zachary Whitlock, could not give myself to soldiering, which inevitably involves the willingness to kill. In that moment it was clear as a sunny day. I wanted to go to Japan, but I would find another way.

Father shifted, turned to face me fully. "Doughnuts?"

I nodded. He started the engine.

The Guardsman stepped toward the car. "Sir?"

"Thank you," Father replied. "It seems our business here is done."

•   •   •

Several days passed. My father returned from a trip off-island and walked to where I was pulling weeds by the porch steps. "Zachary, I ran into Michael Walters at the committee meeting. I told him the subject of Seagoing Cowboys had come up, and I remembered he'd once looked into it, but didn't go. He said, yes, he and his wife had learned she was expecting."

Mother came out of the house, drying her hands on her apron. My mother was always creating something, in the kitchen or at the sewing machine or the spinning wheel.

"He said, though, that his cousin plans to make one of those trips. Maybe Poland."

"He meant John?" Mother asked. "John would join the Coast Guard?"

"No. As it turns out, Michael said that requirement was suspended a few months ago, now that the war has been over this long."

"Do you mean that to volunteer, to be a Seagoing Cowboy, a person *doesn't* have to join the Coast Guard?"

"That's my understanding, Zachary. It seems an obstacle has fallen away." He clapped me on my back, as if I were his equal, something my father up to that point had never done.

My parents didn't know I had mailed my Heifer Project application *before* I went to the Coast Guard station. Also, I had worked through the first three chapters of *Japanese for You*.

I had not received a letter from the Heifer Project, though. No call. No telegram. Eventually, I learned there wasn't a place for me on the team. But Mr. Schmoe said he was putting me on a waiting list.

Disappointed, I tried to squash the feeling, like a spoiled copy of a school assignment, smashing it into a smaller and smaller ball, aiming it toward a wastepaper basket.

My father said he was sorry. "I know you were looking forward to this. But there's still the Young Farmers Leadership conference."

"Yes, sir."

Three days went by. One afternoon I was reading in my room when Mother called up to me from downstairs, "Zachary! Telephone! It's Floyd Schmoe."

I took the receiver, expecting another "Sorry, buddy," but instead, "Ben Davis won't be travelling with us. His father had a fall, and Ben took over the lumberyard yesterday. Zachary, you're up! Pack your bags!"

"Yes, sir! Thank you, Mr. Schmoe. Thank you! I will see you soon!"

Should I tell him my bags have been packed for more than a month?

CHAPTER SEVEN
Noisy Nuisances

Wiping my forehead with my arm, my sleeve comes away soiled with straw and blood. But this was a simple birth. Relatively. Not the doe's first. First births can be demanding, difficult for both mother and baby.

"Zachary! You're bleeding."

"Lee! Hey! No, really. That's from the birthing. It's kind of a messy process."

"All right, sure. How did it go?"

"Easy."

"You don't say. I'm going to get a towel for you. Or better, several."

"Thanks. The towel I keep in my kit was useless after five minutes. Twins!"

"That's great! I'll hurry."

Lee comes back with a pile of ragged-edged towels and a waxed paper-wrapped packet. "Andy stepped out of the galley and asked me to bring this to you."

"Thanks! Still warm!"

With my mouth watering, I unfold the wax-paper. The bread is misshapen. Peanut butter and jelly ooze out past the crust.

Lee's expression is apologetic. "Uh, I had to carry the sandwich under my arm."

He stays while I clean up the gear. At a moment's notice every item must be ready to use again. But never in my life have I wanted a shower so much.

Forkfuls of straw are coaxed into the pen's corner. Oval-shaped droppings slip through pitchfork tines and lay on deck smelling like—nothing. The droppings of a healthy doe give off little or no odor. The manure, I will dump into the ocean. We have no practical way to transport it for use in enriching fields in Japan.

A merchant sailor I've heard people call Manny leans on a railing watching, scowling. He appears to be talking. His mouth is moving, and he gestures.

The usual rhythmic growl comes from the guts of the ship, as some call it. From the innards, the workings of the ship.

Manny shakes his head, says something. Still, I can't make out his words. "Excuse me?"

He shouts. "Blamed noisy nuisances, aren't they? A man can't get no peace."

Maybe he's tired. I am too, but I couldn't let that go. "These does are yearlings, far from a home they will never see again, taken from the mother doe who bore and raised them. They're corralled on a ship that is never quiet, on an ocean that is never still. They are going into labor early, and they don't understand what's happening. Imagine what they're feeling!"

"Not a chance. Goats are goats. I know they used to be kept on ships for milk, and I know their pens were kept in the chief petty officers' quarters, and I know calling it the goat locker is a joke and a tradition. But it's got nothin' to do with me, you understand? I hate 'em. I might could put up with one goat on a ship, but this stinkin' horde don't belong on a ship. Nope. Not for no reason. I am counting the days until you are gone."

Then he left. He could have left sooner, as far as I'm concerned, but once again I find myself asking, "What have I done? How did I get here?"

•　•　•

A pail of warm milk swings on its handle, the last to be filled from the day's second milking. My hands are tired. Once this pail is emptied, I'll hit the galley for a cup of water and a roll left from the noon meal.

A guttural scream stops my heart. Tackled from my left, I stumble and drop the pail. Turning, I am face to muzzle with a buck rearing to his full extent, cloven hooves sharp as knives coming at me. Jerking back, I fall, landing on my hip, peering up at the big goat's belly.

Angry words turn the air blue. Leather-gloved hands shoot out, grab the buck's horns, and wrench his neck. The beast lurches sideways, then bolts toward the pen's gate.

I hear a wheezing noise. It's me.

A man stands, hands on his knees, inhaling, exhaling. He picks up the now-empty pail and rights it.

"Blast it all, I gotta chase after that devil. I tell you," he pins me with a glare, "I am counting the days."

Two sailors take hold of the buck and work a rope around his neck.

A *whoop*. "We got him, Manny!"

Manny lifts his hand. "Thanks, boys!"

He turns to me. "You could've been injured, permanent. Where was your head, letting that brute get the drop on you?"

That brute came out of nowhere. But I'm not going to argue. I don't want Manny to think I'm ungrateful.

Floyd enters the pen, closes the gate and twists two lengths of wire to secure it. He comes to my side and steadies me as I get up. Then, with a hand on my shoulder, guides me to a hay bale to sit down.

Has anyone ever been killed by a goat? A ten-foot-tall he-goat? I remove a piece of straw from my mouth and another from behind my ear. My wrist is bleeding, and I move to suck it clean, then realize how I got that cut and think better of it.

Floyd extends a handkerchief.

I take it. "Thank you."

Manny pulls off his gloves, reaches out.

Floyd shakes his hand, commenting, "Goats are mean, sometimes."

"Sometimes?" Manny wipes his hands on his pants. "Yeah, they can be ornery."

"The bucks."

"Yup. The does, too. I seen a mama goat butt another's three-day-old kid clean across a pen for coming too close. Fierce. Mothers look out for their own."

"You have some experience with goats."

"I do, and I don't want no more." Manny leaves, closing the gate behind him.

Floyd sits down beside me. "That dust-up was unexpected. Or not entirely. I know a little something about goats. But as much as the man says he despises them, he shows up just when he is needed, where, as far as I know, he has no reason to be. What could we take from that?"

I am gulping air as if I've been rescued from drowning. Between breaths I say, "He hates goats and doesn't care much for people?"

"What makes you think he doesn't like people, Zachary?"

"He doesn't like me?"

"Again, he didn't have to be here. He knew you would be working nearby."

"He doesn't hate goats?"

Laughter. "Maybe the man's feelings are mixed. Conflicted. People's actions are based on what they believe to be their duty, sometimes determination, stubborn persistence, or guilt. Justified or unjustified. Envy, ambition. Often, it's something from their history."

Floyd fake-punches my arm. "Zachary, that must have been quite a fall. What hurts?"

What hurts? My pride.

"Maybe I was careless. Where did that buck come from, and I had no clue?"

"What were you thinking about at the time?"

"Lunch."

"Hunger will do that to you. I've got to get to the bridge. I have paperwork for the captain."

"The bridge? The bridge really interests me. I know it's closed to most of us, but I'd sure like to see it! Every kind of math must come together there. Trigonometry, geometry, calculus, algebra. I think it must be the greatest evidence of what math can do."

"I seem to remember trigonometry is indirectly what got you here, Zachary."

"I guess you are right! That's what I was doing in the big leaf maple that day when you were at our house. Trigonometry homework. Thank you for pointing that out! I kind of like thinking of it that way. None of us would be anywhere without trigonometry, I guess."

"Agreed. You are absolutely correct. I dare say the captain might find a way to make an exception for you in any case."

"That's okay. I don't want anyone to think I'm getting special treatment."

Floyd makes a brief bow. "As you wish."

CHAPTER EIGHT
Betrayal

The date is burnt into my mind: August 6, 1945. I was fourteen.

I got an early start that morning, cared for the sheep, changed clothes, and rode my bike into town. I needed to take the article about the Young Farmers Showcase to *The Bainbridge Communicator*, then get back home and study recommendations for keeping animals calm at judging events.

Mr. Edwards said the report looked good, and he thanked me.

I asked, "Could I get change? I'd like to get a *Post-Intelligencer* for my father from that new machine out front."

"Sure, Zachary." He handed me the cash box key. "Go ahead and get that yourself. It's a dandy gadget, isn't it? People are worried they'll be the end of newsstands, but I see an opportunity to get the paper out to more readers. Imagine being able to buy a newspaper at the gasoline pump when it's closed? Now that's something."

I can hear *even now* what happened next. I can see it. Feel it, the way you experience an awful dream. I walked across the polished wood floor toward the yellow box that held cash for the day's transactions. I had just aimed the key toward the lock when Mrs. Edwards called out. "Walter! Come here! Walter! The U.S. dropped a bomb on Hiroshima!"

The words took the air from my lungs. I turned and walked toward the office, my vision veiled and the atmosphere quivering, like a mirage.

Step by step, with that nightmare feeling of exerting great effort, yet finding it impossible to get where you are going, I reached the office door, the cash box key biting into my palm. Mr. and Mrs. Edwards stood side by side.

Mr. Edwards leaned toward the teletype machine. "A single bomb? What kind of bomb?"

"It says, 'an atom bomb, with power the likes of which the world has never seen. Hiroshima decimated.'"

Mr. Edwards looked to the floor, shook his head, and took Mrs. Edwards' hand. "What more are we capable of?"

I felt small and unsure. Like a little child again. One bomb. A whole city. "This has to be the end of it, right?" I asked. "Hirohito will surrender, won't he?"

Mr. Edwards frowned. "Japan hasn't shown fear or reluctance toward death, Zachary. Children have been forced into military service. Japanese pilots become weapons, flying their planes into ships at sea. Maybe Japan will surrender. But if not . . ."

A whole city. Thousands of people. Dead, injured, if alive, maybe soon starving. Who would help them?

I put the cash box key on Mr. Edwards' desk. "Excuse me. I have to leave now." I hurried out the door.

The Civil War. The Spanish War. World War One. World-wide wars. Barely a heartbeat between them.

Too late. It was too late. It was too late *before* I had the thought. Foundations for peace must be laid well in advance.

Looking back, I realize the pressure in my chest, the inability to breathe, was anger. I'd given thought to the topic of war. Battle strategies, many are based on math. Motivations? Some wars were based on disagreements people couldn't even name anymore. That made me angry. Why was nobody learning from past wars? What was it exactly that stood in the way of peace? Who would think of using such a weapon, a weapon which obviously had been in production for . . . for how long? What kind of mind would create such a thing? I was angry at Japan for its brutality toward us, for calling down devastation upon innocent citizens, babies, children, men and women, old and young. But now for them I felt—what? Betrayed by my countrymen?

I rushed out the door, jumped on my bicycle, and rode to the edge of town, past homes, toward the fields, pumping with every ounce of my strength. I rode onward, across a wooden bridge and onto an up-sloping unpaved road, unaware of blurred images, ditch banks, hedgerows. I tried to escape the explosion threatening my mind, my body. I did feel betrayed. The worst betrayal, unthinkable, as if Fumio suddenly stopped being my friend. I believed the U.S. had progressed beyond mass killing. My legs began to shake. I dropped to the ground. Betrayal. That is what I felt. I felt betrayal.

Below me, to the southeast, Eagledale Harbor was cluttered with its usual water taxis, ferries, and tugs. On the docks, groups of workers surged and ebbed. To the north, Winslow Shipbuilding throbbed with the sounds of metal and fire, addressing a backlog of damaged vessels, victims of the Pearl Harbor attack. To the north, Whidbey Island Naval Air Station, the growl of patrol planes' flight, the rumble of military jets taking off.

A wail pierced the air. The noon whistle at the dock. Mealtime. People were going to eat their lunches as they always do, not knowing that maybe hundreds of thousands of people lay dead, and we Americans had killed them. When the air in Hiroshima became fire, when people could no longer breathe, how long before their hearts stopped? How many were orphaned? How many babies cried for their mothers?

CHAPTER NINE
Typhoon!

"Zachary!" An urgent whisper wakes me. "Zachary!"

The ship is moving oddly. Something is off. Didn't I fall asleep just a minute ago?

"Huh? Who?"

"It's me! Eddie! I need your help!"

"What's going on?"

"A birth, Zachary. The doe is in a bad way!"

During birthing season, a goatherd's, or drover's, sleep is sporadic. The Heifer Project's plan to time breeding of does to deliver after arriving in Japan apparently has come up against nature taking its course.

From what I've been told, goats are not as tender toward newborns as sheep are. I don't know why. But when I think of the onset of calamitous pain and confusion, and the youngest mothers with no idea that this torment will end and the reward will be a new life, what right do I have to assume a doe will meet my expectations? I crawl out of the bunk and follow Eddie. We enter the pen.

"Hey, kid." Manny. His habit of calling me kid is getting old.

"Dark as a tomb," he says, "but no trouble finding you. Must be the smell."

Right. The smell of blood and fear. Her first delivery, and this doe is in trouble.

"Yeah. Just plain goat reek is bad. But in a storm, everything that smells *stinks*. Eddie maybe knows, but I gotta tell you, kid, a typhoon is heading right for us. Could be a big one."

Eddie frowns. "You sure?"

"Sure, I'm sure. How you gonna earn that next certification if you can't read weather?" Manny shrugs. Frowning, he rubs his back.

"Okay. You're right. Hey, I've got to get to the engine room. Sorry I can't stay, Zachary."

"So, a typhoon. Mr.—" I don't know what to call him. "Manny" seems too familiar, and "sir" wouldn't be right. "Uhm. Manny. When do you think?"

"When do I think? Always." Manny laughs louder than his joke warrants. "What do I hear? That's based on reports from young hotshots who got it from the ship's radio. Time was, though, and still is, you gotta read weather! Storms can turn on a dime. On a pinhead. So, you want to know when? An hour. Two hours if we're lucky. Kid, you're going to have something to write home about."

Sheesh. Does he think I'm a tourist?

"You ever seen a ship stand on its nose? 'Course not. How 'bout standing on its tail, huh? That's what'll happen. Nose. Tail. Nose. Then it's like going full speed down a highway and the guy at the wheel stomps on the brakes. Lucky if you don't get your neck broke. A guy told me, he's on his bunk, top bunk, and *thunk*, he's sliding across the deck. He slams into the lockers, and he stays there the rest of the night, 'cause why bother, ya know?"

Sure. "We'll be heading for the nearest cove, then, right? Any port in a storm?"

"Any port? Hah! You really are green, aren't you? Bet you don't know about Lucille."

The clerk who loaned me a wastebasket when I was suffering seasickness comes into view. Jameson. "Oh, yes. She was a terror of a typhoon. Good evening, gentlemen."

"Gentlemen?" Manny laughed. "Yeah. Hey, Jameson. I gotta be going."

"Zachary, good to see you've rejoined the living. Could you use help? Why don't I go get a broom?"

When Jameson returns, he clears away soiled straw. "Lucille was a typhoon that three years ago played havoc at Buckner Bay off Okinawa. Winds ninety-plus miles per hour. Waves thirty-five feet high. Twelve ships sunk. Over two hundred grounded. Thirty-six men killed, forty-seven missing, a hundred badly injured. Sixty planes damaged. Base buildings, Quonset huts, eighty percent of military housing. Destroyed.

"Most of the ships that got damaged slipped anchor, swung wild, rammed into each other. Those ships weigh more than six thousand tons, even without cargo. Typhoons don't grant favors. A port must be of a capacity to allow a ship far enough inside for adequate protection. We're nowhere near a harbor like that.

"Anyway, the ship would be at risk from debris ripped loose by wind. You've seen photographs of cyclone damage? House roofing. Whole trees. Flying cars. We'll outrun the storm if we can. If we can't, we'll ride it out."

Ride it out? Maybe this is where the cowboy part comes in.

The ship rocks. I hear my heart pounding. Two hundred twenty-seven goats, mostly pregnant does, a handful of newborn kids, not to mention twelve paying human passengers. The captain will see to their welfare.

The goats are my responsibility.

The birth proceeded while we were talking. Whatever trouble the doe was having when Eddie came to alert me appears to have resolved. The doe has called on inner strength. Her name comes to me. Petra, after the ancient city carved into sandstone, the "Rose City." In this light, she almost does have a rose tint to her fur.

I clean up the kid: One, clear the mouth and nose. Two, when breathing is normal, tie off the umbilical cord, snip it to three-quarters inch, and dip it in iodine. Three, towel dry, especially important in case of cool weather or a stiff breeze.

This ended well. In a difficult birth, or a multiple birth, the mother might become exhausted, and if the baby is not freed from the birth sac, licked clean, and its nasal passages cleared by the mother, if no one is there to help, in other words, the baby dies. Sometimes I wonder if domesticated animals perhaps have lost part of their original instinct.

"Zachary, you okay with putting this broom away? I'm a few minutes late for my shift."

"I don't mind at all. Thanks, Jameson."

A moment later, Captain Townsend arrives. In the trouble light's artificial glare, his face is shadowed. I don't like to think how I must look. The amniotic fluid as the kid struggled to emerge, gasping for air, birth sac fragments, all on me now.

"Whitlock." The captain enters the pen, resecures the gate. "I heard one of our charges was delivering. Do you have everything you need?"

"Yes, sir. Thank you."

"You've been informed concerning the oncoming weather?"

"I have, sir, yes." The pen is a disaster, but a thrill runs up my backbone at the newborn's mewling. Stroking the doe's nose with one finger, I speak without thinking, "You did great, little mother, *Petra*," then expect demeaning laughter.

Instead, the captain says, "She did. I'd ruffle her ears if it wasn't so hard to get blood stain out. Goats, once you get to know them, are somewhat like dogs, aren't they?"

"They are. Friendly. Most of these goats seem to like people, well enough. But they sure can be mean to other goats."

He shakes his head. "But not these little ones. As they grow older, where does the orneriness come from?"

Good question.

"Get yourself into shelter, Whitlock, when—if—you can." Captain Townsend salutes, which I return with a bloody hand to my forehead, and he walks away.

The wind blows warm. The ship rocks hard. To stand without holding on to a rail is difficult. The newborn kid is weak. The doe shows fatigue.

Sitting on a bale, I rest my back against a bulkhead.

Mama doe begins licking the baby. Perhaps fifteen minutes pass, the kid stands, tottering, ducks its head under Petra's belly, and soon finds its first meal.

Lee arrives a few minutes later. Floyd is with him, and a sailor I've seen talking to Eddie. The three men adjust their stance to absorb the ship's movement.

"Trouble's coming." Floyd looks toward the sailor. "Any ideas, young man?"

"I'm Andy, sir. This is my first voyage, my first typhoon, but I want to help. I'm off shift, and I'll do whatever I can."

Floyd reaches out, shakes his hand. "Thanks, Andy. Two of our volunteers are still suffering from seasickness. Your assistance is most welcome."

I want to stay with Petra and her newborn, but all hands are needed to keep the herd safe. I have no idea how we're going to do that. Moving even a dozen sheep in a trailer behind a small truck is difficult. The sheep are restless. The trailer rocks.

Goats, as I know them now, are more excitable than sheep, and this isn't just a bad road. This is a typhoon. But maybe it will miss us. I've read that the air smells like ozone before a typhoon. Sweet, like clover. I smell oil, diesel, rust.

I put aside what I cannot do. I cannot get the goats under cover. To herd them down to the tween-decks, the *twin-dex*, would take too long. Also, they would be in danger from equipment and items of cargo we do not have the time or means to secure.

The goats will be safer toward the center of the main deck than at the gunnels or outer railings, which aren't substantial enough to keep them from being thrown overboard. I pace among the pens, trying to picture the ocean writhing in thirty-five-foot waves, but I can't imagine that. Should I move the goats closer to the bulkheads? How would we hold them there? Though the fence panels are portable, I don't have time to reposition them.

I explain my plan, we discuss details, and Lee and Andy go to their chosen areas of responsibility. Floyd heads for the bridge.

The wind spikes without warning, slams me from my right. I grab for a handhold. The railing gives way, but not disastrously. Wire? Twine? Tape? Where would I find those items?

We must shift some goats away from the edges and into the pens nearest the ship's center, using whatever we can find to reinforce the panels. Crowded goats, however, are unhappy goats. Unhappy goats can be cantankerous, dangerous to each other and to humans. Anyone volunteering to help must be warned.

But wait! I remember Jessica mentioning that all herds of goats have a herd queen, a doe of regal behavior who rules the roost, so to speak. A herd queen even tests food, tasting it and deciding if other goats should eat it. Herd queens often chase away predators and defend kids who are the target of too much teasing from others in the herd. Maybe a former herd queen has come to this ship and is ready to accept the crown, or a young doe who will come to recognize her status as herd queen. I've noticed a doe I privately labeled "Her Majesty." She is a beauty. Haughty. She can, occasionally, be kind, also. When I carry feed or minerals into the pen, she comes to me and, when I set it down, hard as it is to believe, she licks my ear. The first time it happened I nearly jumped out of my skin. But I've come to expect it. She walks with me as I carry feed or water into the pen and pushes other goats aside. I'm hoping she will recognize herself as herd queen and lead the way.

I've moved Amelia, Petra, and their newborns into the safest pens. Hay bales will keep them nearer the ship's center and if fence panels do shift, bales will lessen the force. We'll arrange a double row of pens along the bulkhead to create more resistance to shifting, leave an aisle, and form another double row of pens. We will do what we can. Until we run out of time.

•   •   •

A pallet bearing four hay bales rises on the cable. I'm up top, working the winch. The ship lurches. The pallet swings wild.

"*Whoa!* Look out, Lee!"

My stomach twists. I have no power over the wind or the pitching of the ship. I cannot control the weight and force of the pallet and those hay bales hanging from the block and tackle.

"Lee, let's move fewer bales at a time and I'll bring them up more carefully. Then, if you do have to duck out of the way, you'll have a better chance of surviving."

My attempt at humor fails. I'd switch places with Lee, but I'm the one who knows where bales must be placed.

"Zachary, I've adjusted my hold on the rope. Ready?" Lee shouts. "Go!"

With a firm grip, I pull as hard as I can, never taking my eyes off the pallet. We will work as long as it's safe.

I doubt we'll have time to move the bucks to a safer location. If we could, we would reinforce the pens standing against the leading edge of the waves. But that would require knowing which pens those would be.

As bad as this morning is, it could get worse, so I take the bandana from the duffel I've shoved behind a bale and jam it deep in my pocket. For my eleventh birthday, my mother planned a Cowboy Party and invited all the boys in my class. She bought a red bandana for each of us to tie around our necks, like Roy Rogers and Gene Autry. We signed two bandanas in ink, one for Fumio and one for Joey Kato, and sent them to Camp Manzanar, where they were held that first year, to show them we missed them.

I keep mine in the duffel with the animal care kit I take to Young Farmer events and, once, to the Evergreen County Fair. The bandana symbolizes to me the importance of team work. Even when, especially when, things get tough.

A lightning bolt slashes the sky, which is heavy with clouds. A low vibration and a rising roar, as much a feeling as a sound, goes through me like a shudder. I tie the bandana around my neck, zip up my coat, pull on gloves.

Radio operators dash to and from the bridge and engine room with, I'm sure, information on the storm's path and intensity, and the ship's systems. A man approaches, shouting, "Heads up! We're diverting east, but as we maneuver, the ship's gonna get a whomping. Multiple times. No help for it!" He hurries away, talks with Lee, then sprints for the bridge.

An unbearably loud sound blares, like a foghorn, what people here call a claxon. We stop lifting bales. Sailors pull knit caps lower, covering their ears, and turn to heavy weather duties at their stations. Passengers have been told to go to their cabins, securing—dogging down—cabinets and stowing loose items.

I will stay on deck with the goats. Lee chooses to stay, too. We survey pens, checking for weak places and, especially, twists of wire, tucking in loose ends. We listen for notes among the constant bleating that signal critical urgency. We eye the ocean as it heaves and spills. We watch the sky.

At each lightning strike, I startle. My ears ring. Thunder reverberates in my chest like the huge drum, the odaiko, which was part of the taiko drumming demonstration I saw when we visited Fumio and his family at Hunt Camp, the internment center we now call Minidoka.

Seawater-diesel slurry inundates us, threatening me with nausea, but I manage to will it away. This must be how it feels to ride a bucking bronco, bareback. Just as I think I've found a secure hold, the ship lifts. Gradually I learn to lean and sway, counteracting the waves' force. It's as Manny said, the ship moves "nose, tail, nose." He didn't say, "hip, shoulder, hip," but there's that, too.

More than two hundred pregnant does endure this without understanding it. Even in that moist inner darkness, unborn kids must sense the extraordinary, thrashing movement. But can they hear the raging waves? Do they perceive images?

I hope there are no births today.

With the thought comes a thin sound, nearly obscured by waves and wind. And again, the threadlike cry. I close my eyes to listen.

As though heaved upward on the back of a monster, the ship bucks. A wall of water surges across the deck. I am left gasping and drenched and cannot see, but I hear the ship's groan. I've read a large ship is a hotel. I've read it is a city. As the ship voices its outrage against the pounding waves, as it shrieks and moans, righting itself after plowing its shoulder into a wave trough, in this moment, I understand. The ship is a body.

Saltwater fills my nose, sinuses, and runs down my throat. I wipe my eyes with my bandana, tie it over my lower face, then double-check the knot.

Lee signals for attention, arms above his head. As I move toward him, the ship's bow rises. I flail but remain upright. The ship drops, another rush of water breaches the bow. A hunk of steel shoots down the slope of the deck. Lee is swept off his feet into the rush of water. The smell and taste of salt and seawater assault me. Again, I brace myself against nausea.

I reach out to him, but the bow plunges, and I don't have a chance of connecting. He shields his face with his hands as his body slams against a bulkhead. He slumps to the deck.

"Lee?" My inclination is to grab him by the shoulders and pull him up, but I make myself wait. "Lee?"

A loud, deep breath, an exhalation. "Huh, wha—?"

"Lee, are you okay?"

"Don't know." But he moves the fingers of one hand and then the other, flexes his shoulders. Finally, he pushes himself up to lean against the bulkhead. I sit down beside him.

"My mother," Lee pauses, "my mother would say, 'That's going to hurt tomorrow.'"

What would my mother say? How would she feel if she could see me right now?

"But I'm okay. I'm all right."

My throat is tight. Words won't come. *But I was so afraid. I thought you might be washed overboard or killed slamming into a piece of equipment. I feel so guilty.*

I feel guilty. *Would you have been out on this deck if it weren't for me?*

But of course, he would. No doubt. Lee would brave this storm and do his best for the animals. For the passengers and crew.

Breathing hard, we sit on the deck watching giant fronds of seaweed and the occasional fish slide by. "Look!" Lee points to a blown-glass ball, a float that would have come free from a fishing net. Blue green. "But the goats. The pens . . ."

We decide to split up. It's a big ship. We agree that if I don't see Lee, if he doesn't see me, at least every ten minutes, we'll "Halloo!"

Alert for the next big wave, I start with the stern where I'm surprised to see, on a ladder, sitting on the bottom step, head down, hands over his ears, Manny. His shoulders shake.

Manny, I know, would not welcome an offer of help.

"Hey, Zachary!" Vernon beckons. "It's okay. Manny is holding his own. I'm checking on him now and again. The noise, the havoc. It takes him back to his time in the war. In the Philippines."

"The Philippines?"

"Bataan. Yes?"

No, but this doesn't seem the time to ask.

"It was bad. Real bad. Look it up in your encyclopedia at home. It'll give you nightmares."

Lightning strobes the sky. The goats' bleating sounds like irón skillets being beaten with mixing spoons. The ship continues to rise and fall, jarring the bones, rattling the teeth.

Me, on the port side. Lee, on the starboard. We continue patrolling pens.

•   •   •

Later—hours? days? Time has been suspended, superseded by the storm. Lee approaches at a run. "Zachary! Hey, Zachary! They're gone!"

"Gone? Who's gone?"

"The twin kids! Both of them!"

Fighting panic, I scan the deck looking for two long-legged kids, striplings, off on an adventure, unaware of the peril. We hurry to their pen. Sections have separated and fallen. Mama Amelia stands shaking, her cry a howl.

I want to drop everything to search for the twins. They are young and precious. But I force myself to think about the other goats. The bucks were left most vulnerable. We should check on them.

We pace without slowing, cautious, alert. Eventually the wind quiets. The ship settles, rocking side to side, then forward motion takes over. The course adjustment has succeeded.

My shoulders relax. Lee signals, nods *yes*, and I acknowledge. The crisis has passed for now, but we know the angry spiral of wind and waves could shift and again take us in its grip.

Now, we must find the twin kids. Fast.

The deck is slick with saltwater and littered with small items of gear. I walk from bow to stern, port to starboard, pausing to secure fence panels, and come upon Mrs. Blake. Her face is damp, not surprising, but her eyes tell me she is crying.

"They're gone! You must help me! They're gone!"

Mrs. Blake seems to be a kind and caring person. But I wouldn't have expected her to be so upset about missing goats. Or even to know about it.

"The kids, yes, that is upsetting."

"Upsetting? Terrifying! On this ship? I don't know where to begin looking."

I'm puzzled, but Floyd approaches. "Mrs. Blake."

Then, to me, "Any word? Has anyone seen them?"

"Not yet," I answer. "I've searched the entire main deck looking for droppings or some clue to their whereabouts."

"Droppings?" Floyd frowns.

Pelting rain blurs my vision. In my mind, I picture the deck. Where would two very young goats be? Remembering the power of that wave pouring over the deck, cascading over the railings, my stomach clenches.

But I hear giggling. The laughter of a child. Or children.

Children! Kids! Is Mrs. Blake searching for her children?

Again, giggling. Now, the harmonium-like tones of a very, very young kid. Then, another, more like a chortle. Coming from my right. The ladder to the tower, partway up. Two little goats. Two little children.

"Mrs. Blake, Mr. Schmoe! Here they are!"

As I approach, the goat kids clamber farther up the ladder. The human children follow, calling after them. "Wait! Wait for us!" More giggling.

A child squeals, a playful sound of delight. But one little goat stumbles, falls down two steps, is stopped by the legs of the children, one of whom falls also.

The situation has become this: Teddy and Cassie and two goats are wedged together in a ladder's narrow space, which at home would be called a staircase. The children are afraid. The goats are confused. The deck, ladder, and handrails are slick with rain.

Mrs. Blake rushes to the ladder. Her foot slips on the lowest step, she catches the railing with one hand and twists downward, barely missing hitting her head. Floyd goes to her and helps her up.

Over the rain, I shout, "Please! Let me go up the ladder! I'm wearing the right shoes."

In fact, I'm wearing the boots I've worn every day since I boarded the ship. Not to have a meal at the captain's table, but otherwise. I give this as a reason for Mrs. Blake and Floyd to let me do this. I can see myself doing it. Quietly. Slowly. Allowing the kids, goats and children, to right themselves as I support them in doing so.

Which is exactly what I do. We shift our weight inch by inch, then by a half inch, then a hair's breadth, Floyd extends his hands to Cassie. She takes hold and he steadies her as she descends one step. I edge past and slip my hands beneath a baby goat's midsection. Cassie goes down one more step, Floyd hands her to her mother. I am able, now, to gently lift the little goat. Those long legs dangle as Floyd reaches out, just as gently grasping its midsection.

The other kid bolts for the tower. Teddy follows. Up to the tower and the captain's bridge. Up to forbidden territory.

"Zachary, hurry! Give the kid to me! Go after the other one! Get up to the bridge!"

I take the steps two at a time. The little goat disappears through the door, Teddy following. I'm close behind, and a moment later, at the bridge's entrance.

Maybe because of the enclosed space or the glare of artificial lighting, the little goat has stopped. Teddy is behind him. Just past the door, I halt, surrounded by banks of gauges, dials and knobs, toggles and switches, insulated wiring, and metal tubing. What looks like telephone handsets hang from hooks. Pings, chimes, and clicks sound unceasingly. Everywhere are squares of enameled metal, printed with item numbers and dates. Equipment certifications.

I am awestruck by the level of skill it must take to guide this huge ship. Will I ever be able to do something that far-reaching, maybe not on a ship, but ever, at all?

"Zachary?"

"Excuse me?"

"Zachary!"

"Yes, sir. Hello, Captain Townsend."

"It's good to see you, and surprising!"

"Thank you, sir. I am sorry. In the storm, they got away from us. I didn't mean to impose."

"Of course not." He laughed. "I must admit that when I saw that little goat scramble in—and, Teddy, hello!—I was relieved to see you close behind. Fourth Engineer Vasquez mentioned that one of our Cowboys was interested in math and anything mechanical. I'm fairly certain that Cowboy is you. We'll call this a fortunate accident."

"Yes, sir. Thank you. I have been curious about the bridge."

"'Bridge' is a broad term, Zachary. Officially, you are standing on the bridge level, in the pilot house. Step over here."

I join the captain, before me an overwhelming vista. Droplets of sea spray pelt the glass, gather, and stream downward. As water does. Below is the deck, the bow section, members of the crew, and from this elevated position a limitless view of the ocean, choppy and alive with whitecaps. And the sky. Unending sky.

"Out there, the area *around* the pilot house is the bridge, sometimes called the captain's bridge. No overhead shelter, so it's not a comfortable workplace. But when necessary, the OOD, the Officer of the Deck, will locate there to control the ship and communicate with the pilothouse, the radio room and the engine room. Sailors might return the OOD's communication using intercoms, voice tubes, or even by yelling through the portlights."

I can't think of what to say. I want to study that view for hours, days. But then comes the sound of a small bleat and a little boy's voice.

"Ayeayesir." Teddy rushes his words, meanwhile saluting a sailor three times. The sailor, grinning, returns the salute, once, and escorts the boy and the goat out.

"We don't encourage visits to the pilot house, Zachary, human or otherwise. Communications codes are kept here. I can't see your presence as a problem, but—"

"But it's a rule," I finish the statement for him. "I understand. I appreciate your patience."

"You are welcome. I wish I could add, 'Come back any time.'"

We both laugh as we shake hands.

"Thank you, again, Sir."

I descend the ladder carefully, aware of the damp footing. The world is a big place. Too big to see it all. But I'd like to see more of it. Bainbridge Island is home. Sometimes, I think the Island is, almost, the world in miniature. A blend of persons from many cultures. But often with an American accent. What would it be like to go to a place where the language was as old as the earth? Unchanged over time? Does such a language exist?

Floyd calls from the bottom of the ladder. "Zachary! Hurry! I've got your animal care duffel. One of the does is giving birth."

Instantly, I remember. The small sound that nearly blew away with the wind. That was a doe experiencing the pangs of an oncoming delivery. I hurry to Floyd. "Where?"

"Not far." He points.

Lee and I had moved the doe to a pen near a bulkhead, bracketed the panels with hay bales, which did not hold and succumbed to the waves and the wind.

Huddled against a bulkhead on a skimpy pile of wet straw, a single hay bale between herself and the open deck, lies an exhausted fine-boned doe, a Saanen, white with no contrasting markings. Beside her, one kid. She struggles to deliver another. I regret the delay, but I run anyway to the head and scrub my hands and arms thoroughly with soap and disinfectant.

When I return, baby number one leans against Floyd's leg, appearing to breathe well. "This little one was suckling when I arrived. Good news, wouldn't you say?"

"Very good news. Colostrum. Crucial for survival."

On my knees, I carefully lift mama doe's head. She has beautiful eyes and long, thick lashes. Like feathers. "How are you, little mother? I'm here to help."

Twins are not uncommon, but her level of exhaustion scares me. Each breath comes with immense effort.

Soon baby number two, a male, emerges into my hands. I lay him beside his mother, give her time to look directly at him, to acknowledge him, then I follow protocol, wipe his face, check airways. The umbilical cord needs no extra attention. I'll stay alert to prevent infection. I watch as this baby, too, latches on to his mother's body.

Lee appears. We use towels to dry and soothe the babies, keeping them near Feather. Yes, I've named her Feather.

I encourage Lee to go to his bunk for some shut eye. He's had a rough night and might need to see a medic.

Grateful the seas are quiet, at least for a time, I hit the head to wash up again, then get into clean clothes and, with two blankets and a pillow, return to the deck to remain near Feather and her two little ones.

I dream of sheep. I dream of Flyer. I dream of Fumio. A broad field. Green grass. We are moving sheep to a less-grazed pasture. When we were still boys. Before everything changed. I hear a small cry.

The dream feels so real.

The crying grows louder, more insistent. I pull myself reluctantly from sleep. It is real. I hear, not a lamb, but a kid. Not from near the bulkhead, where Feather and her twins rest. Sitting up and throwing off the blanket, I take the flashlight from under my pillow, turn it on. A kid, shivering, mewling, stands in the circle of light.

This must be Feather's first kid, a kid she delivered alone before Floyd came upon her, which means she had not twins, but triplets. Somehow, I misunderstood that. She must have been terrified. A storm without and a storm within. Not once, not twice, but three times. Now this babe has been wandering around alone for too long and is in trouble, needing immediate nourishment. He stands still while I move slowly toward him. I see no fear.

At home I rigged a rack to hold bottles for nursing, four kids at a time, and put it with my gear, planning ahead. The bottles are glass. Between feedings, they are cleaned with scalding-hot water. The attached nipples are a black, pliable material, similar in appearance to a mother's teat, soft for a kid's mouth, but a hungry baby can yank the nipple off the bottle and then, the milk is lost. I am watchful. I'll do what I can.

I'm glad for the colostrum stored in the galley's freezer, but I wish I had met this little one sooner. If he survives at all, Baby Number One will be bottle-fed. Lots of work. Work I'll be glad to do. Grateful to do. For certain, Feather will reject him.

•　　•　　•

The worst of the storm's violence has passed, we are told. Feather is standing, two of her kids toddling beside her as expected, since fifteen minutes after their birth, nosing her sides, her belly. A good indication that I can safely leave them alone and look after the rest of the herd. The firstborn is asleep, nuzzled against a wool blanket. My own. It's the best I can do.

Evening has come. Each sailor's limit has been tested, and the emergency met without hesitation. Strain is etched on every face. Determination and satisfaction, too.

At this point, I've visited every pen, made repairs on some, and carefully studied our charges. Their fatigue shows. Most have rearranged their bedding to their liking. I think of myself at nine years old, willingly making my bed every morning, then coming home from school to see my mother had "neatened" it. Although I quickly came to expect it, I also routinely sighed like a steam train and pulled out the tucked-in corners at the bed's foot. I did not like tight covers. My feet required room. My toes were sensitive. Goats, evidently, have preferences, too.

•　　•　　•

Hours now have passed since the births of kids Number Two and Number Three. Feather stands, as do most mama goats, directing, nudging them, bracing herself to bear their weight as they lean on her while learning to suckle. Number One has taken milk from a bottle three times at this point.

Kids that cannot nurse from their mother must be bottle-fed, four to six ounces, four to five times a day. I've learned from Eddie that Saanen goats are preferred because the does are heavy milk producers, more so than most breeds. We're fortunate to have "bonus milk" from Amelia and Petra stored in the freezer in the galley.

Early on I asked permission to keep extra milk in the galley freezer. I was told to speak to the chief cook. Very territorial, I learned. That was a tense conversation. But a sailor slicing potatoes nearby started laughing. "What's the hang-up, Carl? Milk for baby goats make you squeamish? Really? You, who I've seen kill a rat with a meat mallet?"

"Shh-shh-shh! Okay! Fine."

I've been bringing milk to storage twice a day, with no discussion of the matter, but Carl began stopping by to watch, smiling, when Feather's kids were being fed.

Hoping to see contentment, I approach Feather's pen. She is lying down in the straw. Looking despondent, anxious. It might be distress over being forced from her home, loss of the comfort of the loafing shed and barn. Possibly nausea from the sea's unrelenting motion. Perhaps something as simple or as elemental as the absence of familiar odors. Or the fact that she's had three births and now the constant presence of babies, and the confusion surrounding the one she does not recognize.

Even providing nourishment for two would deplete her nutrition stores. I'll need to stay by her side as much as possible while keeping a close eye on the others to hopefully prevent any more rejections from occurring.

CHAPTER TEN
Right Man at the Right Time

"Floyd, whatever happened to the Blue Box? Is it in a museum somewhere?"

"Or a junkyard, were you going to ask, Zachary?"

"I wasn't, but is it?"

"No, but the old behemoth was using gallons of oil when I drove it."

"The Blue Box is a vehicle?" Andy asks.

"You could call it that." Floyd chuckles. "A bus belonging to a community center in Seattle. The automotive shop class at Stonyridge High School took it on as a project, so it runs well now, but it's still a rather shocking blue."

"*And* the Blue Box was used for a Youth Project headed up by Floyd. A group of us teenagers did upkeep on properties owned by Japanese American families who got interned during the war. Sometimes we had to repair houses and farm buildings because they'd been damaged by vandalism."

"Vandalism? While they were imprisoned?" Andy.

"Angry people venting a misplaced desire for revenge," Floyd says.

"Kept us busy, unfortunately," I add.

"Where is it they were sent?"

"Our next-door neighbors, the Miyotas, were sent to Manzanar, in California. All our Japanese American neighbors were sent to California. The Miyotas' property? We didn't leave it vacant. My brother Jacob is ten years older than I am. He has a degree from Pacific College, and last year he became the principal of the elementary school. Jacob is married. Some of you know about my brother's wife, Jessica, who is a veterinarian."

"Ah, that explains a few things."

"Yes. When a ewe from our flock looks like she's having trouble delivering, Jessica comes, and she lets me help, so I know a few strategies for difficult births. Jacob and Jessica were able to move into the Miyota house and, fortunately, it was never vandalized.

"My friend Joey's home was abused, though. Insults painted on the walls. Doors jimmied open. Windows broken out. And it rained overnight. Neighbors didn't know what had happened until someone saw it on their way to work. Inside walls, soaked. Rugs, ruined. Drapes—my mother tried, but she couldn't repair them."

I feel my voice getting louder the longer I speak, so I stop, take a deep breath, which feels caught in my chest. I try to steady my insides. I didn't know I had been so bothered by the events of that day. "Local people pitched in when they realized what had happened. The paper printed an article and a few of the people who did the vandalizing got reported. The sheriff arrested them. The same sheriff who was with the FBI when they raided Japanese Americans' homes. A couple of the vandals went to jail."

"So," Lee says, "was their stuff ever returned?"

"Nope."

"And the government sweeps up your neighbors and moves them—"

"Under armed guard."

"Under armed guard? To live in shacks in the middle of nothing?"

"Yup," I reply. "That sums it up pretty well."

Floyd shifts his position again, stretching his feet out in from of him. "Desperation can inhabit deceptively ordinary places, my friends."

•   •   •

Remembering those days now, I can almost feel the roughness of the bark against my back. The maple tree outside my window has always been, to me, a part of my bedroom, as a porch is part of a house. I can climb through my window and into it any time I want. I've sat in its branches in all kinds of weather, but I especially like being there in the rain. A pine tree would break the fall of raindrops. A maple tree doesn't, but it slows them. The whisper of drip, slip, drip is quiet music. Subtle, always changing. When it's raining, I don't write. I just listen.

I've seen drawings of crow's nests on ships. Lookouts. The maple tree is that, too. Fumio was sitting in the tree with me when he saw our neighbor, Mr. Harvey, pull into his driveway and talk urgently with his father. We didn't know what had happened, but we knew it was something awful. Fumio slid down and took off for home, followed by Flyer, faster than I've ever seen them run. That was the morning Pearl Harbor was bombed.

The day after Fumio's house was raided by the FBI, he came to our front door, knocked, and spoke to my mother, as he always does when he arrives, then came out and climbed into the tree. Flyer waited below on the grass.

Fumio told me his house felt strange since the agents came and went through their belongings. He didn't know how to describe it, he said, but something was off, like they took something, something more than the few items they confiscated—one of which was only a cookbook—and left something worrisome behind.

For a while we just sat there, not talking. Then, my mother leaned out the window with cookies tied up in a cloth napkin.

We thanked her. I took a cookie, broke it, and handed half to Fumio. As always, he gave half of his half back to me. We sat quietly for a while, thinking and chewing. Then we talked about becoming blood brothers, like we knew kids sometimes do. Fumio didn't like the idea of swapping blood, so instead we stuck our thumbs together and said we were brothers. Forever and for always.

•   •   •

A few days have passed since I told my long story. For some reason it has lingered with me. Maybe the memory was stirred up by the typhoon. Maybe it's a sign of missing Fumio, of missing home.

The evening meal in the mess is over. After checking on our new mothers and their kids, I come upon Floyd again, sitting on a hay bale, facing the ocean, and I sit down nearby. "Hello! How was your day?"

"Busy!" He hands me an apple.

"Thanks!" Positioning my hands carefully, I squeeze the apple, twist, and *snap!* It breaks into two pieces. I offer half to Floyd.

"Very impressive!" He laughs. "But no thanks. I've noticed that after lunch you share an apple with the three little mothers."

"Yes, and breaking it makes it easier to flick out most of the seeds."

"Strychnine. Right."

I break one of the halves in two, drop three quarters of the apple into my pocket, and bite into the remaining quarter. It is, after all, a gift.

"The ocean is continually in motion," Floyd says, staring out. "Busy. But sometimes, it looks lonely. There's something about . . ."

I know, I think but don't say.

"It's a fact. The ocean may be full of life, but it is lonely. There's only ever one ocean in one place. No clan. No kin." Floyd looks at me as if to say something more, but he doesn't.

Maybe I'm bothering him. But he did have that apple and obviously did not plan to eat it himself. No one has joined us. The silence grows heavy and begs to be broken. My thoughts are as restless as the ocean's waves. "I know Ben Davis is your friend. It's too bad he's not here."

Floyd glances at me, returns his gaze to the ocean. "He's missing a great experience. But I'm sure Ben's more concerned that his father can rest, knowing the lumberyard's well-managed."

The words are out before I can stop them. "And I was a ready substitute."

"What's that?" Floyd frowns.

"I'm filling Ben's place. I'm a substitute." My stomach feels prickly, crowded with sticker burrs. From nowhere comes an image of the treacherous plants that grow along the edges of gravel lanes. We call the sharp-pointed spines *goat heads*. I know I'm not really talking about Ben

Davis, but I can't blurt out that technically speaking I'm a substitute in life. I'm a substitute child. Maybe I'm just too sensitive. Sometimes I think so.

"Oh? *Hmm*." Floyd stands. "I'd better get going. I have letters to write. Zachary, Ben Davis doesn't know a thing about goats. For this job, you were the right man at the right time. And you can take that to the bank."

• • •

Approaching Yokohama, energy surges. Sailors move briskly, falling to their tasks. Maintenance crews jump into action. Today they want their ship to shine. Officers' shoes click smartly against the deck, in the passageways, and up ladders to the bridge as information is routed, preparations made to connect with tugs, to go to dock, and to greet port authorities.

I catch the spirit and look at my charges from a new perspective. Will these Saanens draw approval from Japan's Agricultural Department? The goats are sure to be welcomed by their new families, aren't they? I don't keep a comb or brush in my kit. To use one with sheep would harm their wool. I find a soft brush, though, to slick straw from the coats of the less tidy does.

Another question looms. Will I be welcome, as someone offering friendship and help? Or assumed to be American and swell-headed, on the winning side of what for them must have been a humiliating war? Check that. Nobody wins at war. Some people just lose less.

Even so, in their place I would be resentful, angry. Suspicious and hoping to find fault.

The Japanese language has been hard to learn, even the little I know. I might be laughed at for trying. And it's written in symbols, none of which I have yet learned to recognize. What if I get lost? I won't know how to ask for help. Who did I think I was, hopping a ship for Yokohama, anyway? Wet behind the ears. And, okay, sensitive. That's me, in Japan. Am I scared? Sort of. Nervous at the very least.

CHAPTER ELEVEN
Japan

Yokohama. Out of my bunk and up on deck early. Ready to go.

My experience since leaving San Francisco plays like a movie through my mind. The overwhelming scale of the SS *Contest*, the broad top deck, the maze of spaces within the tween- and below-decks. Memorizing how to get from one location to another. I've mostly gotten used to the smells, the noises, existing on checkered sleep. I've experienced a glow of competence like never before. I survived our brush with a typhoon, as had the dozen passengers, the crew, and the herd. Minus three. In the storm, we lost three bucks. Also, though, six births occurred while we were at sea.

In Yokohama, I expect off-loading to be the same as loading, but in reverse.

However, in San Francisco the animals were herded by experienced stockpersons from a loosely structured parking area, into a confining, controlled space, gangways leading to pens on a ship's deck. While, in San Francisco the goats may have shown initial resistance, once inside they were mostly docile.

Today, different story.

The ship's human passengers wait, we hope, in their cabins or, at least, at a safe distance, as the goats' exit is supervised by, well, *sailors*. Few merchant marines have experience in herding. We are inundated by animals blasting objections at the top of their lungs, jostled by does, and rammed by the bucks' hard heads. The clatter of hooves roars like thunder. Like a typhoon. Surrounded by so much metal, sounds reverberate, assume weight. I am pelted by the racket and my teeth hurt.

The goats will be quarantined by Japan's agricultural department before being sent to livestock breeding stations, and from there distributed to families.

I'm excited and anxious and worried. Feather is still not doing well.

A pregnant doe presents special demands. One is extra calcium. Supplements. Bags of minerals got stowed in the twin-dex during the storm by shipmates who helped us clear the deck of potential hazards. In the chaos, I overlooked that fact and missed providing a very important element that Feather needed.

Thankfully, so far, she and her kids have survived.

This evening, Floyd will bunk in the barracks near the dock. He has the shipping and registration papers, and he will be part of the team accompanying the goats to their destinations. Afterward, he'll spend several weeks in Hiroshima. Floyd plans to talk with people in positions of local civilian authority to learn what they feel is important in constructing the houses he plans to build for those without homes after the war.

When Fumio heard I'd be going to Japan, he contacted relatives, and I was invited to visit and stay in their home. Before the war, Mr. Yamamoto was an officer in a bank. Now, during the U.S. occupation, he does clerical work in a government office where his broad understanding of English is helpful. I've looked forward to meeting the family.

Fumio told me it would be polite, when I meet Jun Yamamoto, to address him as Mr. Yamamotosan and, later, I might be asked to call him Uncle, which is "Ojisan." That is usual, Fumio said, among persons who are close friends of the family if the man is older, even though he is not *my* relative.

The beautiful doe, Her Majesty, leads the way as the goats are loaded into transport. They may now be under the care of Japan's agricultural department, but they are under the oversight of Her Majesty.

The volunteers who never got over their seasickness took the first nonstop ship sailing for the U.S. this morning. Later today, Lee will board another for San Francisco. Feather and her three kids wait near the ladder to the captain's bridge. Otherwise, the last few goats have been removed from the ship. I watch the departing herd, feeling loss, as I would regret seeing a relative depart after a week-long visit.

We volunteers traded addresses with some of the crew we've come to know. "I might make it up your way some day," Eddie said, and Vernon said he and his wife had talked of finding a comfortable place to put down roots and that Bainbridge Island sounded hospitable.

We've been told officials plan to arrive after the goats are off-loaded, and, sure enough, approaching now on the gangplank are men wearing suits and hats and well-shined shoes. One gentleman wears a clerical collar. Waiting to greet them are Floyd and Mrs. Blake. Cassie and Teddy are nearby.

"Papa!" a young voice calls. Then another, "Father!" Teddy and Cassie run down the gangplank. They appear almost effervescent. I imagine a rainbow of joy glistening in the air above their heads. Mrs. Blake waits, a quiet smile on her face, dabbing her eyes with a handkerchief.

To think what this family have sacrificed, putting everything at risk to stay strong and maintain their values. And *me*, what did I put my family through? What were my reasons? My desire for my first honest-to-goodness travel experience. To work on a big ship. Regardless of the chance of killer storms or unexploded mines floating in erratic ocean waves. To arrive here, in a place where I know maybe ten words of the language, and I am to walk among people who have no reason to like me, even to tolerate me.

Floyd beckons from the deck. "Zachary! Lee! Please join our discussion!"

Formal introductions are made. I am surprised when no one gives even a hint of a bow as Fumio's family would. Floyd asks, "Zachary, will you please fill us in on the doe and three kids? And the potential problem you mentioned."

"Yes, sir." I turn to include the representatives. "One of the does, Feather—" to which Floyd chuckles—"yes, sir, I've named her. She is, as you heard, the mother of three kids, and she needs special care."

"The doe is sick?" The question comes in English.

"Sir, she is not sick with anything contagious, but weak because after her delivery she needed extra minerals that were stowed for safety during the typhoon. She needs a special diet for a few days. Also, she is anxious and confused because of the travel and the storm. She got separated from one of her kids and now does not recognize the baby. He must be fed by hand. I have a bottle rack." I realize I'm saying too much.

Floyd speaks up. "This young man has experience with animals such as goats. He has built a device which holds bottles of milk when the kid cannot take milk from the mother."

"I see. That would be useful."

"Perhaps your animal specialists have something of the sort?"

"Maybe, but as you realize, they are extremely busy. This worries me."

"Sir," I can't stop myself from interrupting, "handfeeding a baby animal is a pleasant job. I've done it since I was six years old." I hope he doesn't think I'm making too much of myself.

Chaplain Blake speaks quietly to Mrs. Blake, then asks, "May I make a suggestion? I am based near here, and Mrs. Blake and our children are visiting for a time. Together, we could feed the little goat. All three kids, if it becomes necessary. How often, young man?"

"Four times a day, sir, for the next two days. Then, twice a day for probably six weeks, but possibly more."

"That is quite a commitment, but a unique opportunity for the children." He looks toward Mrs. Blake.

"Could this young man teach us what must be done?" she asks.

Since Floyd has the use of a car, it is decided we'll accompany the Blake family and Feather and her kids to the agriculture station, and I'll teach the children to feed . . . little Star. Yes. I have named another goat.

My shore pass is in my wallet, along with the Japanese currency Father surprised me with. I guess he must have made the exchange on his latest trip to Seattle. I hadn't even thought about the need to exchange my American dollars. He wouldn't take my cash in trade, saying we'd settle up later. I know my father well enough to know that meant that he had decided to support me in this endeavor and providing me with Japanese currency was his way of saying, "I approve." Since money was involved, and he and my mother made all financial decisions together, that meant I had her approval, too.

The milk bottle rack and three glass bottles are in my duffel. I'll visit the ship's galley, take the bonus milk from storage, and hope Carl will part with a bucket of ice.

•   •   •

At the agriculture station, I'm greeted by Dr. Masuda.

"Dr. Masudasan, I apologize for my hurry, but I brought goat milk for the kid requiring handfeeding, and it must be refrigerated. I also have a supply of frozen milk."

"Certainly, right away."

With milk storage arranged, we enter a well-ventilated and lighted space where Feather and family are penned. Workers in white coats bring in hay bales. The twine on one bale is already cut and flakes of hay are being pulled apart. Straw is piled loosely in the pen's corners.

I'm shown where I may attach the feeding rack to a fencing panel. I take the rack from my duffel and begin setup. Teddy and Cassie watch, Teddy visibly vibrating with excitement.

A few tools are always in my kit but, having none, I ask a lab worker for wire, then cut six lengths to attach the backplate to a panel's metal bars, being sure to tuck in wire ends carefully. Jerking on the apparatus, I check stability, make adjustments. Then I slip a bottle into an opening.

"Isn't that too tall?" Cassie asks. "It's over the little goat's head."

"That's a good question, Cassie! The rack should hold the bottle above Star's head so he will lift his head to suckle. That is what he would do to feed from his mother. Goats have four parts to their stomach. The first part, the rumen, isn't ready yet for food. With his head up, the milk skips past the rumen and goes to the second, third, and fourth parts of his stomach."

"Four stomach parts? I could eat so many cookies!" Teddy rubs his stomach, and his father ruffles his hair.

I pour six ounces of milk into a bottle, secure the rubber nipple, and slip the bottle into the slot. Star does not approach. I squeeze a little milk onto my second and third fingers and lightly touch his muzzle. A pink tongue flicks out and he mouths my fingers. With only a little more encouragement, Star is latched onto the rubber nipple. I am relieved. This was a big understanding and Star worked it out so quickly.

Splash. I flinch backward. The rubber nipple is in the bedding straw beside my feet and milk covers my shoes.

"Oh!" Mrs. Blake gasps.

Startled, I stare at my shoes. I might be imagining it, but I think I hear Feather thinking, *Haha! Look at that!* As I pick up the bottle, retrieve and replace the nipple, the children giggle and Chaplain Blake covers a smile with his hand.

It had to happen sometime. "Cassie, Teddy, I'm sure Star is very hungry this morning." I can't hold back my laughter, now, and I hear lab workers' laughing, too.

A young man brings a cloth. I wipe clean my shoes.

"Even if we're careful, this can happen. Until we're sure of our skills," I glance toward their parents, "we should divide feeding into two portions. We need to make do with the stored milk we have, which isn't as much as I'd like."

"I might have a solution for that," Dr. Masuda says. "I've inquired but found no herds of goats nearby." He looks toward Floyd. "That does not surprise you, I'm sure. However, not far from the station is a dairy with a fine herd of Holsteins. It is owned by a family open to our advice and also helpful to us. Cows' milk can be fed to the kid?"

"Whole milk, yes. If evaporated milk is available, it's good to add that. Protein and fat content are important. I know you have access to complete information, and the milk I brought from the ship should be enough to get little Star through for a time. Handfeeding might be necessary for as long as twelve weeks. It's possible, though, that Feather will come to accept little Star sooner."

Floyd is part of the group escorting the Heifer Project goats to their new families, and he has meetings to attend. He goes to the car, and the Blake family and I walk from the agriculture station together. On the landing, Chaplain Blake asks if I'd like to hear how the little goats fare. I write my address on a page from the reporter's notebook the Edwardses at the *Bainbridge Island Communicator* sent with me and hand it to him. He gives me a card from a case he pulls from his jacket pocket. We promise to write. Feather and her kids are in good hands.

Tomorrow, I will be picked up by Mr. Yamamoto after spending one more night in my bunk on the SS *Contest*. But for now, I'm not scheduled to be anywhere. And I'm not in charge of goats.

Near the water's edge, a trail extends from the station toward a few small structures, each fronted by a service window. Sailors and, maybe, office staffers wait in loose lines. Aromas wafting my way are inviting. Seabirds' cries, the salt-tinged air, and the sound of an occasional ship's horn encourage a slow pace. I find myself leaning against the back of a bench, watching terns dive for their dinner.

A man passes, walking with a cane. He doesn't speak but dips his head. I acknowledge the gesture and return my attention to the sea.

"Konnichiwa." A young boy.

"Hello. Konnichiwa."

The boy steps closer.

"Thank you. I can speak American. Sir, do you know God?"

"Uhm, good morning. Why do you ask?"

"You are American. You are not a soldier. So, I think you are a church person."

He thinks I am a missionary. The U.S. Occupation. Only military and missionaries can enter the country. Do I know God? *Well.* It isn't that simple, but I ask, "What do you need?"

"Will you tell God, please, I am sorry?"

The boy's face is small, but not like a child's. His dark eyes are too big. His chin is too sharp. His cheekbones jut. Much of his scalp is marked with broad, livid scars. He looks almost like a skeleton.

"Why not tell him yourself?"

"He would not speak to me unless he forgives me. Because I am a thief."

"You are? What did you steal?"

"A piece of bread, and cabbage leaves already fallen off. Brown from bugs."

"So, you took food. That doesn't mean you are a thief. Sometimes, stealing food is what one does. To stay alive."

"Maybe I would not die because of hunger. But my brother, Hayate, he is sick. Like this."

The boy places his hand on his stomach. Mouth stretched wide, he bends forward twice, three times, emitting an awful sound. He straightens, nods. "I think he needs onigiri." Onigiri. Rice wrapped in nori, seaweed.

I think about what it felt like to be seasick. Dim light through small windows. The ship bucking and rolling. Rows of bunks. Mine damp with sweat. The smell, the sound of retching. Goats. Misery. I had no idea what caused the brother's illness.

"Hoshi! Hoshi!" A woman's voice. "Please come here, now!"

I turn toward the sound and see a woman, her clothes hanging on her, too large for her frame, her head covered by a scarf that drapes forward, hiding much of her face.

"Yes, Miss Bea!" he calls. "I am sorry, sir. Miss Bea needs me."

"Hoshi, wait! Can you tell me your full name?"

"Hoshi! Where are you?"

"I must go."

The boy runs toward the woman's voice.

And so, I cannot help. I cannot help this child or his brother.

A wind lifts, heavy with odors of rust, diesel, and charcoal, and I am thirsty.

Standing before the window of a booth with a placard, "We Speak English," I order and pay, and the vendor hands me a bottle from an aluminum tub filled with partially melted ice. Cold water drips down my wrist.

"Excuse me, but do you know that little boy?" How do I describe the child? "He—"

"I saw. I do not know him."

"His brother is sick? The boy, himself, appears ill."

"Yeah. You'll see that here. You know, March ninth."

He goes to a case of soft drinks and, his back to me, begins wiping the bottles with a rag.

"Excuse me?"

"March ninth, nineteen forty-five."

Expecting an explanation, I wait, then realize he's ignoring me. And March ninth? Doesn't ring a bell.

• • •

The ocean is gray in the evening light. Sounds behind me are blunted by the surging sound of water passing beneath us, around us. I've been told many sailors hear voices in the water. I do, now. I hear the voice of the little boy, Hoshi, asking me if I know God. I hear him ask for onigiri. How do I put in words my pain because I could not help him?

So much sorrow. I am only one person. I feel like a moth, throwing itself against a window, again and again, which comes to nothing but broken wings.

Of course, my wings are not broken. I've had a fairly easy life. Am I fit to meet the problems of the world head on? I don't know. When will I know?

"Zachary! How did the rest of your day go? Did you have a good time exploring?"

"Floyd! Oh . . . well. Anyway, I thought you were heading north."

"I am, but I'll leave tomorrow morning. I need one more signature on this paperwork. Red tape." He chuckles. "And you? A monkey wrench in your afternoon?"

"Yes. I hate to admit it. Honestly, I did want to see the real Japan. But so much of what I've seen so far is loss. Devastation. Destruction of livelihoods. Evidence of death."

I tell Floyd about the little boy, Hoshi, his worry for his little brother, and that he, himself, appeared to be suffering. "He was called away by someone, a Miss Bea, before I got his last name. I asked a beverage vendor nearby about the child, saying he seemed troubled. The man answered only, 'March ninth, nineteen-forty-five,' and turned his back on me."

"I've learned," Floyd says, "that those most affected by tragedy find it painful to talk about it. So many people are in need of a meal, of shelter, of confirmation, simply put, that they have value."

"It's a setup for failure. To care, I mean. So much suffering, and I came face to face with it today."

"Neither you nor I can do all that is needed, Zachary. Each day we do what we can and, every day, vow to do better. We can feed the children within our sphere, perhaps at times pushing those boundaries, and tend their wounds. We can try to provide some modest sort of shelter. In the past few weeks, you yourself have helped successfully transport a large herd of goats, assisted at births and shown little children how to feed the newly born."

"Yes."

"All in balance, true?"

I have no answer for that.

•   •   •

"Mr. Zachary Whitlocksan." Jun Yamamoto is well-dressed in tan slacks and shirt, and a light jacket. A dark straw fedora deflects the day's heat. "My family looks forward to your visit." He hands me a small book. "A gift. *Maps of Japan.* We hope you find this useful, although we plan to escort you wherever you wish to go."

The book is slightly worn. It has been used, and I will value it more because of that. I return his suggestion of a bow. "Thank you, Mr. Yamamotosan." I take from my duffel's side pocket a packet of a dozen postcards, professional photographs of "Seattle's Most Significant Buildings and Bridges." The Pioneer Building, 1891. The Alaska Building, 1904.

Smith Tower, 1914. The Fremont Bridge, 1917. Seattle's George Washington Memorial Bridge, 1932. Intended for tourists but, I'd been advised, welcomed as a gift. "From myself and my family, sir."

He accepts the gift with both hands. "Thank you for your kindness." Again, the suggestion of a bow. "We will enjoy these photographs together, this evening, then display them in our kyabinetto."

Mr. Yamamoto indicates a compact beige car. He opens the trunk. After slipping the book of maps into my pocket, I stow my gear and head for the port side, then adjust course. I am in Japan. The passenger side is starboard.

"Within an hour's drive are a few famous castles. Also, on our route to my family's home, you will see temples large and small. Temples are everywhere."

"I would like to see temples, either large or small, thank you, Mr. Yamamotosan. Are we allowed to go inside?"

"Temples are for the people. Small temples might remain open all daylight hours. Larger temples, more ornate, might require that you be accompanied by a guide. I am speaking in general. Many sacred sites were destroyed in the past years."

"You are speaking of," I pause, the words hard to say, "the atomic bomb."

"I am speaking of the air raids. Of firebombing. Here," he gestures, "is a temple with a small waterfall garden. For contemplation."

I want to ask, *firebombing*? But the temple door is open, and Mr. Yamamoto is entering.

The temple face is constructed of stone. Carved images of cherry blossoms ornament the wooden double doors. We exchange shoes for cloth slippers, step into a dim space awash with calm thick as velvet. Mr. Yamamoto turns right and stands against the wall. I follow and stand beside him.

A bell sounds, deep and mellow. It sounds again. Now, an insistent *trinnggg*, like finger cymbals. Once more, the deep-toned bell. A voice, chanting. Silence. Those I can see bow their heads. A few moments pass. We step out, regain our shoes. The light is blinding.

"Time has passed quickly," Mr. Yamamoto says. "We might visit a larger temple tomorrow."

Before entering the Yamamoto home, I again exchange my shoes for cloth slippers from a basket near the door. I am directed to the otearai, "to wash up."

For the evening meal, the table is furnished with beautiful dinnerware. On every plate a steamed trout, whole. A bright green vegetable, shredded. Rice, served in individual bowls. Near each, a small, shallow cup for shoyu, which is soy sauce, and chopsticks.

Standing behind the chair indicated to be mine, I nod deeply. "Thank you for having me in your home."

"We are honored, Zacharysan. Please, I would be glad if you would call me Uncle. *Ojisan*. We welcome you to Japan and to our home. Itadakimasu. Please. Eat."

After a few minutes, the Yamamotos' son, Akimitsu, maybe twelve years old, excuses himself, goes to the kitchen, returns with two forks and two spoons, and hands me one of each. After pouring shoyu into the little dish, he passes the container to me. Akimitsu picks up a fork, then, and resumes eating.

•   •   •

I took advantage of the laundry before leaving the ship, so my clothes are clean, but when I take them from my duffel the next morning, they are wrinkled and, with the humidity as it is, trying to shake out the wrinkles is futile. I'm embarrassed and my face warms, so now I am double-embarrassed. I had wanted to make a good impression.

Activity in the kitchen is quiet and orderly as the table is set for the morning meal. No one seems to notice my clothes need an iron and ironing board.

Our breakfast consists of soft-cooked eggs and rice. Akimitsu pours green tea over his rice. After I eat half my portion, I add green tea to what's still in my bowl. I'm used to sugar, sometimes cinnamon. This is different, but good.

Mr. Yamamoto, Ojisan, asks if I'd like to visit the Minegishi Watermill. It's very old, he tells me, and one of only several to survive out of hundreds that once existed. He and others interested in the area's history meet regularly and work to protect it from falling into disrepair and being destroyed.

Soon, we are in the Yamamoto's car. Jun drives through an area of mostly small residences, then turns onto a lane that runs along the Nogawa River. Finally, he pulls onto a graveled parking area near a sign, "Minegishi Watermill," and we join a small group of people.

Mr. Yamamoto, Ojisan—do I call him this in public?—introduces as the group's leader a woman wearing sturdy gloves, dressed much as my mother does for gardening. I watch to see if a handshake is proper, then merely nod deeply and am greeted with a smile. She speaks to the group, outlining the day's work.

Jun excuses us and becomes my tour guide. "The Nogawa River," he points, "is the source of water drawn by the water mill to operate its wheel. Once used, the water is returned to the rice fields you see there." He indicates a house that once belonged to the mill's owners and tells me that silk moths were raised in the attic of the house, as was common in that day. Their cocoons provided winter income.

Turning to the two-story wooden building that houses the mill, Jun uses a diagram he pulls from his pocket to explain the mill's intricate arrangement of gears, shafts, and pestles, most of which are made of wood. He speaks of the water mill's blades, arranged in a large circle, slanting inward. Although made of pine, which is durable and water resistant, blades must be replaced every few years. It's enjoyable work, Jun says, a sort of ritual: the scent of the wood, the sound of the plane as shavings curl away, and in the background, the old blades telling stories to the new.

Ojisan directs me to the water mill's entrance, and we step into a space dim except for shafts of light streaming through square openings in the walls, cutting pathways through the dust-filled air. Beneath my feet, wooden planks tremble. The posts in this structure have once been tree trunks. From what forest did they come I wonder? Resting my hand on one, I slow my breath and close my eyes to listen without expectation, and hear a low, persistent groan, and a dull *thump . . . thump . . . thump*, and birds singing from the rafters.

Turning before me is a water-powered wheel, fifteen feet in diameter, crafted by hand in 1808. It's a turbine. After one hundred forty years, the Minegishi Watermill still processes rice, wheat, and buckwheat. The SS *Contest* is a steamship, which is what those letters stand for, and is powered by water turned to steam. Once again, a turbine. The watermill is a work of genius. The *Contest*'s array of equipment, navigation devices, technologically advanced systems, altogether are a similar work of genius, both of which are possible because of trigonometry, because of math.

•   •   •

On the return to the Yamamoto home, we find a parking place on a narrow street lined with shops. Open fronts show brightly colored fabric, paper goods, a few items of apparel. "You might choose gifts for your family here," Ojisan says. "The goods are not as plentiful as before the war, but I am sure you will see something nice."

The silk is expensive, but my mother will enjoy even a small piece. I'm shown a lavender-colored section, already cut and priced. At this moment I *am* a tourist. For Father and Jacob, I buy packets of rice paper, and for Jacob's wife Jessica, a small fan and display stand.

The shopkeeper packages my purchases in brown paper tied with jute string. He dips his head. "Arigato gozaimasu."

I dip my head. "Dōmo arigatō."

At the door I ask, "Was that right, Ojisan?"

"It was, yes. Trying to be respectful is always right."

We spend the evening talking. Akimitsu is eager to hear about the SS *Contest* and, especially, the typhoon. The Yamamotos are glad to have news of the Miyota family, Fumio's parents, his little sister Kimiko, and Margaret, born at Camp Minidoka, now a toddler. In spite of my effort to resist, I begin yawning. Ojisan goes to a chest and takes out a blanket. "An extra," he says, and then shows me where I will sleep.

A lamp, a water jar, and a glass, placed on a chest of drawers. Hooks on the wall for hanging my clothes. A tatami mat, a pillow, two light blankets. A slightly opened screened window. A note, "Welcome to our home," written in English and Japanese.

•   •   •

The next morning, carrying the book I was given, *Maps of Japan*, I enter the kitchen.

"Have you found a place you would like to visit?" Ojisan asks.

"If it's not too far, I would like to see this park." I point to it on the map.

"Not far," he says, "and there is a waterfall where we might take a few pictures. I would like to send your family a photograph of your visit to Japan. Perhaps you would enjoy going by bicycle? The weather is expected to be fair." He turns to his son. "Akimitsu, would you like to come along?"

In a neatly organized storage shed, we each choose a bicycle of the right size.

Ojisan sets an easy pace, riding a little in front of me. "The park is in an area that was spared."

I come alongside. "Spared?"

"Spared from the firebombing, three years ago. It remains a place of peace."

The park is surrounded by a hedge. The gates are iron, plain, functional. A man who appears to be an employee empties a large garbage can into a bin. He acknowledges us with a lift of his hand as we pass.

"I hope we see a kiji," Akimitsu says. "The kiji is Japan's national bird, Zacharysan."

"A green pheasant, very beautiful." Ojisan says. "They roam free, those that have survived. Careful of their surroundings, if disturbed, they hide in hedges. Sensitive to tremors, they are more alert than people to coming earthquakes. It is said that green pheasants have sometimes saved human lives."

The waterfall is a cascade of silver. In the pond below, koi swim, orange, black, and more silver. We linger. A family comes to the falls as we are about to leave. Ojisan asks if they would please take our picture. A boy, maybe twelve, is eager to help. Afterward, he hands back the camera and Ojisan offers a fifty sen bill which I know to be worth half a dollar. The boy glances down and waves his hand *no*, politely refusing payment.

Ojisan will send the film home with me, he says, since there isn't time to develop it.

Near the exit we pass a small structure. "A tea house," he says. "We might stop here for a time."

At the entrance, up two steps, we pause by a low cabinet, exchange our shoes for cloth slippers and wait for acknowledgement. I study the building, its materials, wood and bamboo. Beautiful lines. No obvious ornamentation. Not as simple as one might think. I am drawn to the details of its construction.

We are greeted by a woman wearing a traditional kimono, the fabric's subtle pattern glowing in the dim light. On her feet, elevated shoes called geta. She directs us to a low table. Ojisan and Akimitsu sit cross-legged on the mat-covered floor, and I do the same.

Tea is delivered to the table, leaves steeping in water that I understand to be one degree below boiling, enclosed in a ceramic pot, and three small cups. After a short time, Ojisan pours a small amount of tea, first into my cup, next, the same into Akimitsu's cup, then his own. He begins pouring again, from one to another of us. The third time, each cup is full.

"It is so all are equal," Akimitsu says. "If the first cup were filled, that would be the least flavorful, the last cup, the most."

Puzzling on that, I recreate it in my mind. Yes, the brew from the first pour has the least exposure to the leaves. This way, Ojisan's way, produces individual cups of tea as equal as can be. If I hadn't seen this, wouldn't I think first was best?

Before we leave, I want to pay for our tea, but Ojisan's payment of the bill has occurred unseen. By habit, I should thank him, but I feel he prefers that it go unsaid.

The lane we follow is narrow, rough, and pocked with holes. Even so, I am glad to be on a bicycle, connecting closely with the neighborhood. Behind several homes are chicken yards, I know by the sound, and by the white feather that floats and turns on the wind, brushing my handlebars. Large plots of vegetables grow in front yards. In side yards, clotheslines. This feels real. The real Japan.

Children laugh and call to each other, taunting in fun. Three children come from a home's backyard. A little boy runs, while looking back over his shoulder, and calling out: "Nyah-nyah-nyah. Ha-ha!" He hurtles forward, not slowing as he nears the lane.

A dull *thud*. My borrowed bicycle's front wheel jerks left. I correct hard right. The wheel loses purchase, and I am thrown to the ground. When I crawl from under the bicycle, a child sits on the lane, crying. On my chin, a burning sensation. I can feel a break in the skin. My hand comes away bloodied.

The child lies on the ground, sobbing. The girl goes to him and says something perhaps sarcastic in Japanese.

A woman, gray hair tied in a scarf, an apron over a dark-blue dress, comes from the house waving a towel. She shouts something. I make out only, "Beast! Rich American!"

Across the street, a woman emerges onto a porch, a baby in her arms. "What is going on? You American? You hurt our children too much already!"

"No!" the girl cries. "The bicycle did not run into naughty Tui. He ran into it! I shouted for him to stop, but he did not."

Ojisan and Akimitsu arrive.

"Zacharysan, are you all right? The handlebars on Akimitsusan's bike loosened. We had to stop."

"Lucky that we had pliers, but, Zacharysan, we didn't see where you left the main route."

A man holding a paint brush comes down from a ladder propped against what must be a garage. "I saw what happened." Then, he speaks emphatically, words I don't understand, and the angry woman goes to the little boy. "You are not hurt!" she says, shaking her finger at him, then helps him up, and they go into the house. The other children return to their game.

"Pardon, please. You are bleeding!" The man—young Tui's father?—extends a cloth dotted with droplets of gray paint.

I turn down the use of the cloth, but with a deep nod, thank him.

We ride on. Children's voices, the sound of full green leaves rustling in a warm breeze, the smell of fresh paint. A memory comes to mind, and with it, I am back on Bainbridge Island.

CHAPTER TWELVE
Yellow Peril

Winslow Elementary School on Bainbridge Island, Washington, USA, where I spent the first six years of my formal education. The dismissal bell's raspy clanging hung in the air. I was one of the students exiting in waves through the double doors and pouring down the steps.

"Race you to the corner!"

"See ya!"

"Not if I see you first!"

Just a usual afternoon.

Four or five guys stood in a knot by the bike rack.

"What the hey?" one shouted.

And another, "Man, oh, man! Zachary's gonna blow his top!"

Pushing through, I saw my bike, fallen on its side. Beside the rear tire a mostly empty can. Paint. Yellow.

A piece of paper was stuffed between the spokes. Words I knew well were scrawled in pencil. *Jap Lover. Yellow Peril.*

So, this. I'd taken some personal razzing in the past, my family even more, but this was at a new level, and brave to do it here at school. With the handkerchief from my pocket, I wiped off the handlebars, but soon my pants and shirt were smeared with yellow paint. *Sorry Mother!* No jibes from my classmates. I heard, "Sorry, man," and "That's a bum trick. Who would do that?"

No question. I knew. So did they. But I just tipped my head a bit.

I walked my bike past a hair salon and a photography studio and across the street from them, Petric's Feed and Seed and the café.

"Zachary! Zachary Whitlock, hold up there!" Mr. Harvey, a neighbor, called to me.

"Yes, sir?"

"What happened?"

My face burned. I hate it when I blush. "Somebody delivering a message, I guess. Again."

"Well, dang. Someone at that school needs a talkin' to. I know it ain't your first go-round, son. These kids ain't impressing nobody."

"Thank you, sir. I just want to get home."

Mr. Harvey lowered the tailgate and, together, we lifted my bike into the truck box. I propped it against a few straw bales he must have been delivering somewhere and used a piece of rope he gave me to keep the bike upright. He pulled a faded red bandana from his back pocket. "Here you go. Wipe off your hands. Not worried about the truck. But your clothes? Your mother's got her work cut out for her."

"Yes, sir. She does."

When the Miyotas were interned, my parents accepted responsibility for their farm and home, and I helped. That meant chickens. My pal Fumio didn't like chickens, although he did much of the work with the poultry. I also found them to be aggravating. They're a little like goats. Chickens look harmless, but then they get it in their feathered heads to turn on the hands that feed them, spread their wings, and give chase. Those talons and beaks, they're no joke.

The eggs they give are no joke, either. Not necessarily year-round, but with a large flock like the Miyotas', there's eggs aplenty. They sold them by the dozen or the flat. Mrs. Torres, my friend Reyna's grandmother, spoke to Mother and offered to act as manager for the chickens, which meant a few roosters, too, and the sale of eggs. Customers were used to getting their eggs from the Miyotas, and that house was better located for customers than the Torres home. So, near the road in front of the Miyota's home, Mr. Torres built a neat stand, painted white, with a sign: Eggs For Sale.

Islanders knew by word of mouth that eggs were still available, and I saw small notices tacked to bulletin boards in Petric's Feed and Seed, and at the gas station. Mrs. Torres and often Reyna gathered eggs two or three times a day. At five o'clock, eggs not yet sold were put in pails and stored in a cool place. On a chilly, autumn-to-winter day, they were placed in a closed cabinet in the feed room. A part of the barn. Not locked. Why should it be?

But someone went looking. And someone found the eggs. I imagine they laughed as they put the pails in their vehicle. Probably about midnight, headlights off, they drove the mile or so to our house. Then they pelted our house with dozens, hundreds, of eggs. I pictured them standing in silence as they studied their work. Transparent whites and yellow yolks, dripping down the siding, puddling, congealing. Next, the tree trunks. Last of all, the windows.

My bedroom is at the back of the house, and I was asleep. So was my mother. Father was working in his study, editing a final chapter in his current book, with Flyer curled on the rug, also fast asleep. Father had no idea what was happening until Flyer leapt up and began to bark. At that point, the car's headlights came on, the engine roared. They drove onto our lawn, gunned the engine and spun out, digging huge gashes, the driver laying on the horn the entire time.

It would be common, I suppose, to wonder who did this and why. Does it matter? If you found out that someone you thought of as a friend had turned on you, that would be terrible. Or, even if they didn't turn on you, actually, but had given in to the pressure of the gang or *the guys*. Would that make it easier to take?

It's hard to stand up for what you believe is right, especially if you stand alone. It's hard if you grit your teeth and keep on doing what you think is right, but the bad stuff doesn't stop, goes on and on. I wonder if it helps, like some people say, to get mad, to let anger fuel your fire. But no matter who plays with it and no matter the reason, fire burns.

CHAPTER THIRTEEN
Firebombing

"Zacharysan?" Ojisan offers his handkerchief.

I thank him but pull my bandana from my pocket, dab at my chin. The bloodstain is faint.

"We can take a shortcut," he suggests, "and get home more quickly to treat your injury."

The lane is dirt, rutted and gouged by the wheels of carts. Our way climbs. At a widened place, a pullout, I step off my bike, one foot on the ground, one still on a pedal. In the distance, Tokyo is laid out before me, a wasteland. The sight hits me like a blow to the chest. Towering hulks of concrete, misshapen metal, and unidentifiable rubble mark what was once an immense business district. Nearer, what must have been houses, schools, and neighborhood workplaces are reduced to charred timbers, window frames gaping. Blackened skeletons of trees stand naked, limbs lifted in defiance.

Ash blows erratically in the changeable wind. My eyes burn. Swaths of the desolation take on a sheen as glass turned to dust mirrors the sunlight, gilding the ruins. And in the midst, from nowhere to nowhere, a bridge.

I spot shards of charred pottery littering the ground, a scrap of chicken wire, a shoe sole, and a small bowl, blue and white. Dismounting, I reach down to pick it up.

"Excuse me," Ojisan says. "I think you should not—"

I straighten. "I am sorry. I didn't mean to keep it."

"You might keep it, as it belongs to no one. But these things are tainted. Perhaps poisonous. Three years ago. May ninth, nineteen forty-five. We cleaned what we could. But it is too much damage to consider."

May 9, 1945. *Too much damage to consider*. A burning sensation travels the length of my spine. *Firebombing*, Ojisan had said. Little more than three years ago.

•　•　•

Mrs. Yamamoto greets us on the front step, then tells Akimitsu that their next-door neighbor has asked him to please help Taka pick grapes, because, she said, they are ripening fast. "They will send grapes home with you. She knows you enjoy them."

"Yes, Okāsama, I will get my gloves and go now."

"Zacharysan needs first aid for a cut on his chin," Ojisan tells Mrs. Yamamoto, and explains what happened.

She brings supplies to the porch. "May I?"

"Thank you, Mrs. Yamamotosan. Yes." My chin is bandaged. It stings some, but my mother says that means it's healing.

Ojisan and I go out to a bench in the shade of a tree.

"The United States holds dire grievance against Japan," Ojisan says, "and I understand that. Japan's people have long lived in absolute deference to the emperor and to their flag. Not as much to the military, I think. But to Japan, their country, they have been loyal."

"Just as I feel toward America."

"But grave errors were committed in the choices made by Japan's leaders, and perhaps by its people, in accepting their leadership. They were allowed little choice, though. When the war was underway, even children were conscripted from their schoolrooms to perform heavy manual labor, preparing for attack. They could not refuse. Also, they were told it would prove them brave, and even be an adventure."

"An adventure. I can see how they might."

"Adults were made to believe it was their duty and if they did not serve, then came great shame. We were at war. But they were protecting their homes, their families. Victory was the only option. I was too old to fight. Of no use. I admit I was glad."

He turns to look toward the neighbors' garden where Akimitsu works.

"Sir, Ojisan, may I ask? You spoke of firebombing. I've heard nothing of it before."

"Certainly, Zacharysan. You know of the atomic bomb, Hiroshima. And the plutonium bomb, Nagasaki. Firebombing came first. Waves of incendiaries were expected to force Hirohito, the emperor, to his knees. Napalm. A sticky fuel-gel that explodes into flame three seconds after dropped on the target and then continues to combust, invented just for this purpose."

A voice from my left, "My otōto died because of napalm." A boy, eight, maybe nine years old, stands holding a small bucket of grapes. I know that otōto means his little brother.

Akimitsu has returned. I assume the boy to be his friend Taka. I flinch, then try to control my shock. The youngster's face, arms, all I can see of him, is reddened, blackened, in patches pitted by deep burns. I am sure he knows I am taken aback. But he offers me a cluster of grapes, deep carmine. Stems gentle green.

I stand, accept the gift with both hands, bow.

The boy laughs. "You do not have to bow to me."

"Okay. I won't." I manage a smile. "Thank you for the grapes. Takasan, right? I'm Zachary."

Akimitsu holds a basin filled with grapes. He extends a handful toward his father.

"My otōto died because of napalm," Taka repeats. "It was the worst day. My imōto," his younger sister, "and I live there now." He points. "With Okasamasan's obāsan and ojiisan." His mother's parents, his grandparents. "And Otokosan." His father. "Otokosan is sick. It was the law that he had to stay behind to fight the fires. But he helps us here as much as he can. With the grapes."

"Your okasamasan?" To ask about his mother is brash, I know, but the subject is open.

"Okasamasan died. We ran, looking for safety," Taka says, and tells me that his baby brother was on his mother's back, in an onbuhimo. Napalm first set fire to the cloth, and then his brother. His mother was burning, too, and could not untie the bindings. He wrapped his coat over his little sister's head to protect her, and held her hand, but, he says, "I was too far away to help Okasamasan or my otōto."

Then, "*Wham!*" Taka bangs his hands together, and my heart slams into my ribs. "Like that. It was too late."

Akimitsu's hand goes to Taka's shoulder. "We have apple juice." They turn toward the house.

Ojisan sighs. "Those not burned to death suffocated. Napalm takes oxygen from the air and leaves behind carbon monoxide. Tokyo, other towns, too, were firebombed repeatedly. More than ten thousand acres destroyed. Sixteen square miles. One hundred thousand people and more. Dead. A million injured."

It is too much to consider.

"We learned the raids were planned, in all details. Code-named Operation Meetinghouse."

"What—? Why—?"

Meetinghouse. "Meetinghouse is what we call the place where Quakers gather to consider the needs and blessings of their community, of their brothers and sisters, of those they know and those they have not yet met. Meetinghouse is what others might call church."

"I did not know that Zacharysan. Operation Meetinghouse." Ojisan shakes his head. "I do not know why they named it so, but in planning the bombings, weather was important. The destruction was much worse because of strong winds, first from the north, then changeable, blowing in many directions at different altitudes, spreading the napalm more broadly."

I am reminded of a verse from the Bible. *The Holy Spirit showed up suddenly, like a rushing wind and with tongues of fire, a sign of God's presence among His people.*

I knew nothing of allegory, symbolism, or story-telling devices back then when I was a kid learning Bible verses, but I know the Quaker God is not a god of napalm. And I do know fire. Fire, on warm, summer evenings, roasts marshmallows that quickly catch fire if I'm not careful. They blister, blacken—

"Zacharysan?"

"Yes?"

"Is this too much?"

"Yes. But it is the truth, and I wanted to know."

Operation Meetinghouse. A travesty. Another blot on humankind.

"We wish not to think about it. But it is always right here." He demonstrates with his hand in front of his face. "Our neighbors' pain. Shopkeepers. School teachers. Grocers. Some of those with whom I work. And how did we escape?" He shakes his head. "It came with the wind."

Akimitsu and Taka appear on the porch. Akimitsu waves as his friend leaves and returns to his house.

"Akimitsusan," Ojisan calls, "will you please help your Okasamasan sweep the mats?"

"Yes, Otokosan." The boy goes inside.

Ojisan continues. He speaks quietly of scorched earth. Mountains of debris. A tumble of broken stone and twisted steel. "Those buildings that were designed to endure Japan's many earthquakes maintain their internal structure but are not fit for use. Stress from the napalm's heat crumbles even stone."

My stomach twists. The gift I gave the Yamamoto family, the packet of postcards, images of Seattle's Significant Buildings and Bridges.

"Ojisan, the packet of postcards I brought . . . This is . . . I am sorry."

"The greatest loss is not the buildings. It is the people. Their work. The children's futures. Your gift is thoughtful, Zacharysan. We know of your family's kindness to my sister's family, and your friendship is of great value."

•   •   •

Jun—Ojisan—and Mrs. Yamamoto serve a special meal on my last night before I return to Yokohama. I use chopsticks as best I can, picking up a fork when I begin to fall behind. Sitting together at the meal and later in the living room, we tell stories of home, and I learn we have more in common than I expected.

We share mailing addresses. I hope the Yamamoto family might want to write from time to time. I tell them my parents would be pleased if they would visit and stay in our home if that appeals to them. Akimitsu shows enthusiasm at the prospect.

I use the Japanese I know, some I learned from Fumio's family, and some from my studies. I try to say that during my visit with their family I had gained understanding of Japan and the world that would stay with me, and that I had stumbled on questions that would follow me throughout my life. The Yamamotos are supportive of my efforts. I tell them I am determined to continue studying Japanese and that I will look for chances to practice.

In my room, the guest room, I lay awake thinking of all I've seen. I remember Ojisan's words, *the people, their work, the children's futures.* I wonder, is there any way I can help?

Finally, a dreamless sleep. In the morning, Mrs. Yamamoto gives me a packet of fruit and crackers for my return to Yokohama. The family gathers in the living room to say goodbye. They seem a bit sad, which strangely makes me glad.

"Okoshi itadaki arigatōgozaimasu," Mrs. Yamamoto says.

This one I know: *Thank you for visiting.*

"Thank you for inviting me," I reply. "I am honored to have been your guest,"

"Mata kite kudasai." Akimitsu smiles. "Please come again!"

• • •

Mr. Yamamoto and I plan to meet Floyd Schmoe at the Agricultural Department's Yokohama Station. We arrive early. I get my gear from the trunk and wave as he drives away.

Inside the station, I lay my duffel near a coat rack. The door opens. Floyd has arrived.

The station director, Dr. Masuda, comes into the front office carrying file folders. "Zachary, Mr. Schmoe! Good morning! I am glad to tell you that the doe, Feather, and her three kids are doing well. Chaplain and Mrs. Blake and their very active children are here, now, helping Kid Number One feed." He pauses, smiles, "Or should I say Star? Come on back."

Past a swinging metal door, Floyd and I slip into white coats. The facility is sparkling, every surface spotless. Even the straw, laying loose in fluffy piles, is golden.

Chaplain and Mrs. Blake, both in white coats, wave as I approach the pen. Cassie and Teddy wear overlong white coats, bunched around their waists with fabric belts.

I come near, then nearer, until I am looking down on a small black and white head and muzzle, a pink nose, and fragile ears that move in tandem with a busily suckling mouth.

Cassie, with one hand, lightly holds a bottle of milk that's resting in the feeding apparatus and, with the other, manages a careful grip on the nipple, watching as the young kid repeatedly yanks on it.

Floyd steps forward for a closer view.

Teddy crowds toward Floyd. "See! Wegettafeedababygoat!"

Teddy bumps Cassie. The bottle is jolted from its cradle and drops toward Floyd's shoes.

So fast it surprises even me, my hand shoots out and the bottle is in my grasp.

"Phew!" Floyd makes a show of wiping his forehead. "Good catch! I'd rather not smell like sour milk in my meetings this afternoon."

"Saves the milk supply, too," I put in. "We can worry less once the little goats are ready for solid food."

Cassie asks, "Like grass? How would we know when they are ready?"

I'm impressed by her question. "After thirty days, but maybe as many as sixty." I glance toward Chaplain and Mrs. Blake. "They will nibble grain, hay, and grass, following their mother's example."

We talk for a few minutes about the process of weaning little goats, then Floyd says, "We should move on." He looks toward me. "It's hard to leave, though, isn't it?"

Dr. Masuda reaches out, we shake hands, and with a nod I acknowledge other workers in the lab. "Thank you for your help and kindness."

I shake hands with Chaplain and Mrs. Blake. Teddy comes to stand in front of me, tilts back his head to look directly at me, and sticks out his hand.

"Silly Teddy," Cassie chides. "Grownups don't shake hands with children."

But I do. Then, I lift my hand toward Cassie, her face lights up, and we shake hands, too.

Retrieving my duffel, I go out the door behind Floyd.

"Do you have time for a side trip?" he asks me.

"Yes, the ship doesn't leave until tomorrow morning."

"You know that over the next several days all the goats will be delivered to their new homes. We've talked about settling them in with their families. Have I mentioned, though, that some of the goats will go to schools? To orphanages, too, Zachary, and I'd like to drive us to one of those, now. It isn't far."

In fact, the drive lasts only a minute. We pull up near a hedge that needs pruning and a rusted iron fence, some of its sections missing. Floyd parks near a gate that stands open, hanging crooked on the hinges. We leave the car but remain near the gate.

I am struck by the dishevelment of the structure before us. But birds twitter. I hear the sound of children laughing, and I hear a woman's voice, singing.

"We will wait," Floyd says, "to be sure the headmistress knows we are here."

Soon, coming around the side of the house, I see a woman, her clothes too large for her frame, her head covered by a scarf that drapes forward hiding much of her face. Close behind her is a little boy. Floyd opens the car door, gets out.

"Mr. Schmoe!" the woman says. "You are most welcome! Come in! Come in!"

"You are the tall man who wears glasses," the child calls. "Did you bring a goat?"

My heart skips. It is Hoshi, who asked me about God. He waves as I get out of the car.

"Miss Bea, there he is! The boy with bright hair, from the dock!" The sound of this child's voice has stayed in my memory. Sorrow. A call for help. His face has been in a shadowed corner of my mind.

"Ah, young man, now I meet the one Hoshi called, 'a child with bright hair.' Young, but I think not a child. Hoshi, please ask Jeanette to prepare a water jar for us. Thank you, dear."

Dear. Miss Bea cares about Hoshi.

"Mr. Schmoe, we are most grateful for the rice and other provisions you brought after learning of our situation, and we are filled with hope for the future, knowing the Children's Home will receive a goat."

"Miss Bea, I have a question for you. I told the people of the Heifer Project I would like to allot a doe to you and to the Shepherd's Children's Home. She gave birth earlier than expected. They agree with that plan."

"So, a doe and, already, a kid?"

"A doe and *three* kids."

"Oh, my!"

"This young man, Zachary, has experience and the three were born safely, although during a typhoon. One little goat became separated. His mother does not yet recognize him, and he must be handfed.

"A family, the Blakes, will be glad to help you learn to care for the baby goats. Mr. Blake is a U.S. Army chaplain. His wife and children are visiting him. I think you will find help from the Blakes to be useful."

I see tears in Miss Bea's eyes. I notice now that she wears a headpiece much like that of a nun, but Floyd did not call her Sister, as Catholic nuns I've met on Bainbridge Island are called. Her hands and wrists are scarred. I haven't been staring, but I turn to study the landscape. My mother would love to take a pair of clippers to that hedge.

"Mr. Schmoe," Miss Bea says, "I hope to meet with the Blakes soon, and if we find it acceptable to share the work of establishing the doe—"

"Feather," I put in.

"Feather! That's lovely, young man, and have you named the little goats?"

"Only one, Star. You'll see why."

Miss Bea laughs. "I look forward to that."

A young woman, Jeanette, I assume, brings a tray with a water jar and three glasses. As she places the tray on the makeshift table, I see that much of her scalp is scarred.

The day is warm. I appreciate the water. Hoshi and, I think, his little brother stand in the doorway, watching. They look much alike, with matching, beautiful smiles.

Once Jeanette, Hoshi, and his brother are inside again, Miss Bea speaks quietly, "We feel most fortunate to have shelter here, donated by the owner of the estate. Perhaps we, the three of us who make up the staff, should have found a way to leave Tokyo sooner. Leaflets were dropped. Warnings to flee. But then, it was too late. Fire spewing from low-flying B-29s, making the heavens hell. We ran. Carrying nothing. It was my responsibility. We didn't have resources. I couldn't find a place for twenty-three children."

"Miss Bea," Floyd leaned forward, "you did all you could with the information you had, with *what* you had. You have been a blessing."

"Thank you for coming, Mr. Schmoe. You, also, Zachary. In showing concern for Hoshi, I think you have been our angel."

"I am glad our paths met, Miss Bea. Thank you for the water."

And for so much more, I think. *Thank you for the care you will give Feather and her kids, for the care you give otherwise homeless children. Thank you for the care of Hoshi and his brother, whom I could not help.*

But I see it now, I did help. Floyd and the Seagoing Cowboys, the people of the Heifer Project, the sailors on the SS *Contest*, and the families who donated the goats, we all helped.

CHAPTER FOURTEEN
Home

Floyd and I drive past the agriculture station and on toward the dock where we pull up near a ship's ladder, I get my gear, then Floyd takes off. Here I am again, a cargo ship's hull rising before me. This is not the SS *Contest*—that ship left port within hours of its arrival—but another C2 freighter, the *Julesburg*, my home for the next twenty days.

At the Ward Office, I check in, get my bunk assignment, then stroll the passageways, learning the lay of the ship. I miss seeing the men of the *Contest*, whom I now think of as friends, but I appreciate the practiced, precise movements of these merchant marines as we prepare to leave Yokohama.

I step carefully, adjusting once more to the motion. Then, a sudden worry: *Am I going to be seasick? Not again, please.* But the nausea passes quickly. Any unpleasant experience is more bearable if you know it will eventually end. The needle's pinch during a vaccination. Birth pangs of does. The growing pains in my legs when I was fourteen and fifteen.

This ship, on its return to the States after delivering goods, is transporting troops to their homes or to new assignments. Not used to idleness, it seems, freedom from duty has some of them pacing or, in groups, talking excitedly. Others appear exhausted. A few lean against the deck's railing, eyes closed. One man's face is wet with tears. He holds a photograph.

"Can I help?"

"Maybe. Thank you for asking. Bereavement leave. My father died. I need to confess my guilt. It's my fault."

Unexpected. "Your fault, really? Is it guilt or sadness?"

"Both. If I'd been home to help with the shop, he'd still be alive. He had a heart attack."

"But—"

"He wouldn't have been working overtime day after day if I'd been there to help. I enjoyed the Navy. The travel. I stayed gone too long."

Stayed gone too long. But how are we to know? What do I say now?

"Thanks for hearing me out. You really helped." He straightened, inhaled deeply, and walked away.

With no livestock to load, I finally have time to take it all in, the big picture. The ocean is calm, and tugboats, compact, muscular, wait to tow us from the dock.

Through my feet and up to my ears, forceful vibrations, an insistent shuddering, metallic clicking and thuds, more felt than heard. The odors of electrical wiring and the tang of steel, heating, coming to life, are as much flavors as smells. A soup of oil, decaying sea life, and sewage rises from the water, stirred by the ship's engine. The departure horn sounds, both triumphant and forlorn.

Underway. A lump in my throat and an ache in my chest, I wave good-bye to Japan.

I have the okay to eat with the crew. An evening meal in the mess on a ship's first day at sea is lively. Old hands tell tall tales.

A few men sing. Then, "Enough of the chanties, maties," a man calls in a broad accent, faked, judging by the laughter that follows. "Any greenhands on board will find out sooner than not that yer full of hot air!"

The meal's last course is a fruit-filled pie, still warm. I thank the nearest cook and take dessert out on the deck. I've met a few of the sailors already. One man plans to sail for five years, then return to his family farm. Another is a poet.

•　　•　　•

Evening, sailing southeast. I sit on deck, legs tucked beneath me, facing the ocean. My reporter's notebook is propped on one knee. I'm running out of pages. My eraser is nearly gone.

I didn't bring a pencil sharpener, and yet I have one here in my hand. Back on the *Contest*, I had once asked in the galley to borrow a paring knife.

"For what?"

"My pencil is dull."

"Your pencil isn't all that's dull if you think I'm gonna let you hack on a pencil with one of my knives. Go find a clerk, for Pete's sake."

As I walked away, he continued to bluster. "No respect."

Jameson was glad to let me use a pencil sharpener. He pointed. "There you go." It was bolted to a counter.

Going out the door, I heard, "Look sharp!" I turned and, just before it smacked me on the forehead, I reached up and caught a small, plastic-cased, handheld sharpener.

Jameson said, "That's actually my own. Go on and keep it. Sorry, I should have given you more warning."

The ship rocks, a gentle motion. I know that behind me, sailors off duty are reading, telling stories. A couple of the men carve. One is making chess pieces he sells when in various ports. For good money, he says.

One man crochets. Many sailors do, he said. And they knit. Useful for making sweaters, heavy with lanolin, to ward off ocean spray, no fancy equipment needed. I'll tell Mother about it, but she probably knows. She's writing a book about crochet, its history and current day uses, and whether it is a dying art or does it have a future?

The sailor said he makes mittens and sometimes caps, too, for gifts. So, I went to my cabin and came back with two dollars. My mother can make her own mittens, of course, but this pair will be, as Floyd said about his name, a conversation starter. When I tell the sailor my mother cards, spins and sells yarn from our own flock he asks, "Does she have a shop? Where?"

I take a half-page from my notebook and give him the address.

"I knit wool diaper covers. The lanolin water resistance is helpful." He chuckles. "My favorite thing to make, no lanolin needed, is crocheted baby booties. Lotta guys buy 'em to send home. Lanolin—the other side of the coin—you know about reloading? That's reusing ammunition by refilling the brass cases. Lanolin is used in the process. So, there's a new market for your sheep-raising business."

I nod and thank him but, no, I don't think that's a new market for us. I wonder if Mr. Harvey, our neighbor who's a dealer of solvents, oil, and grease used in equipment repair, might have use for a similar product. Maybe I'll run it by him.

•   •   •

The Ward Office clerk walked by while I ate breakfast in the mess. "You're from near Seattle, right? You gonna send a message informing someone about your arrival time? Don't wait until the last minute, please."

I hadn't considered my way from port to home yet, expecting to figure it out when the time came. I guess it's time. Sure. I'll send a message so Mother can quit worrying, Father, too, though he might not admit it, and let them know I'll be home in a week. In San Francisco, I can hit up the Greyhound, get a ticket, and, as I've now heard it referred to, "ride the Dog" home.

As I come out of the Ward Office a day later, a message home sent, an orange cat sits, eyeing my movements. I've encountered him before. He might be lying on the deck, eyes closed, rocking with the waves one moment, and exploding into action, streaking after vermin the next. This morning, he sits in a sunbeam, fur glowing. I reach down to scratch him behind the ears, but quick as a blink, he's gone.

"That cat's on the job, you know. Besides, he's particular about his friends. Pretty sure he smells goat."

I laugh, then turn to see a gray-haired sailor, thin as a reed, and tall.

"He has high standards, does he?"

"Yes, he does. And you, I understand, are nothing but a Singing Cowboy. Do you play harmonica? Guitar? Yodel? A regular on stage at the Grand Ole Opry is what I hear. And a Jap lover to boot."

I don't stop to take a breath, I react, fueled by fury, maybe for the first time ever. "Yodel? I'm returning from a trip as a volunteer *Seagoing* Cowboy, not a singing one. I suspect your term, 'Jap lover' is meant to insult me."

"You got it in one, Dick Tracy. I hear you are a Bible thumper, too."

"What's your problem, Ivan?" A younger man, an officer by his uniform, approaches. "You know this guy's a paying customer? Captain wouldn't like to hear you're being rude."

"He was on the *Contest* delivering a giant herd of stinkin' goats to the Japs. The same Japs who bombed us to hell and killed our boys and we bombed back. He wasn't even getting paid for it. Some kind of goody-goody."

"So, Ivan, he tapped you on the shoulder and proceeded to share this information? He looked you up to tell you this?"

"No—"

I move to stand facing both men. Something shifts in me, like a boulder that has all this time been unmovable, like all of my muscles are suddenly on high alert.

"Ivan, is it? Seems to me, Ivan, *sir*, that you are surprised, angry even, that I would give my time to deliver goats to Japan. I have no idea why you might think this is any of your business. I was taught to respect my elders, but what you just said to me is not deserving of respect. Goats do stink, the males, anyway, and people stink, too, something I keep learning over and over on this trip. Farmers gave those animals to Japanese families in need. They received no money for that, either. They care about people who were harmed by a war they didn't start and didn't want.

"You call me a *Jap lover*? Well, sir, you are not very inventive because you are certainly not the first. I did fall in love with people while I was in Japan. Some of them were children covered in burns from warfare my own country carried out. My best friend comes from Japanese heritage, but he and his parents were born in the United States. Still, they were locked up for years in ramshackle camps for no reason. His grandfather was *recruited* to come from Japan to work in a lumber mill. Work. Any idea what kind of hard labor it is to work in a lumber mill? You ever do that kind of work?"

The young officer reaches out as if to shake my hand. "Sorry, man. Ivan was running his mouth off. Uh, my apologies, but I don't know your name."

"Zachary Whitlock. From Bainbridge Island, Washington. A Quaker. A Conscientious Objector. To most people, a friend."

Ivan, with a *harumph*, walks away.

A handful of people who have collected around the scene begin to lightly applaud. Two men walk up and shake my hand.

"Zachary Whitlock, leftover waffles are stacked on a platter in the mess."

The officer lifts his hand in *so long*, a gesture I return before heading for the mess. Standing up to Ivan has made me hungry.

• • •

Five days later. A veil of fog hangs unevenly. Ships' horns sound. I am with a small number of people gathered on deck as our ship makes its way toward San Francisco's Golden Gate Bridge. I find my hand over my heart. Many sailors and soldiers salute the flag flying from the bridge's apex. The sun breaks through, drawing exclamations and cheers. In a deep voice, someone sings "My Country, 'Tis of Thee."

As much as I have enjoyed my travels, the sight of this bridge sends a thrill from my toes to the top of my head. I am sure this is one of the most beautiful sights on earth. Unquestionably, it will aways be that to me.

On the deck of the SS *Julesburg*, in San Francisco's harbor, I am just another passenger. My duffel slung over my shoulder and my gear bag in hand, I lean against a railing and watch the tugboats' maneuvers. A shout goes up as the ship shoulders into its berth.

Sailors stand back, and so do I, as non-military passengers make their way down the gangplank.

From ships on each side of us, cables shriek, passing through winches, as the off-loading of cargo goes into full gear. I think of my own struggle with a much smaller block and tackle moving bales of straw before the typhoon and am in awe of the clockwork precision I see around me. The constant rattle, *boom*, clank, rumble, and slam has me marveling that any item will be delivered unscathed, but I know this is how the system works.

Beyond the ships' massive hulls, angled ramps, gangways and a maze of boardwalks, on land, to my right, a broad field rises. Small trees grow bravely through masses of brush. In a moment of silence, I hear the familiar *Hello* of a goat. Then the light tones, a chorus, of does. Among the bushes, munching like little machines, a small herd of goats works at landscape control. Who'd have thought I would see them here today?

The roar of a motorcycle's engine being kickstarted into action brings me back to my location. My stomach growls. I ponder the likely whereabouts of the nearest Greyhound station.

The parking area below me is filled with every variety of vehicle: cars, vans, trucks small and large, a tractor, several bicycles. Sunlight glints from the hoods and roofs of some. Others wear a solid coating of dust. Work transportation in a dry climate. I head down the gangplank carefully, watching each step, not yet sure of my land legs. Once on solid ground, I look up and see coming toward me . . . my parents? *Mother and Father*? I stare, stunned, confused, my mouth involuntarily agape. How are they here? In San Francisco? Am I dreaming? Is it an illusion, a mirage?

"Zachary! We hope you don't mind." My mother reaches out and for a moment her arms are around me. She smells like roses. For some reason she looks smaller, almost fragile. Did my absence have so much effect on her or am I seeing her differently?

"We were able to get away for a few days," she says.

Father and I shake hands.

I search for words. Then, "This is amazing! How did you manage it? You can't believe how much I have to tell you."

Father laughs. "We hoped you might. When we received the ship's message, we knew we wanted to hear everything. Everything you've experienced. We figured a road trip was a good way to make that happen."

"While your experiences are still fresh in your mind," my mother adds. She takes my coat from over my arm, letting her hand linger on mine for a moment. My mother isn't usually one for touching. "It's warm in California!" Her eyes shine.

I pick up my gear. Father takes my duffel and, walking ahead, glances back. "Hungry?"

"You know, I am." I feel, in fact, a bit lightheaded, not from hunger, I think, but surprise.

"We have a meal waiting in a park with a view of the bridge. Will that be all right?"

"Better than all right."

Across a span of grass, I see a bulky, blue bus lettered on the side, "Seattle Youth Center." Floyd Schmoe's Blue Box.

"There you go!" my father says. "The center's board was happy to rent it to me."

"Jacob and Jessica send their love," Mother says, steps near, straightens my collar and pats my shoulder. Once again, I'm taken slightly aback. My mother has always been loving, but not outwardly affectionate. After weeks of handling goats, human touch feels doubly strange, especially coming from my mother. I find myself having to swallow against a lump in my throat. When was the last time I cried?

The door of the Blue Box opens. Mr. Miyota comes down the steps, turns to help Mrs. Miyota as she joins him. Next, Kimiko takes the first step, then pauses, a quiet smile on her face. I am struck by her almost grown-up appearance, ten years old, as were Fumio and I when Pearl Harbor was bombed and his family was pulled by the roots from their home and farm, from their community and their hard-built lives.

Our world was changed, Fumio's and mine, but not our friendship. The words we spoke as we sat in the maple tree, the day after the FBI raided his home, come back to me: *Brothers. Forever. For always.* I know those words now to be an unbreakable oath.

Fumio stands at the top of the steps, holding five-year-old Margaret's hand. Margaret, undoubtedly, has a mind of her own, but I am taken by surprise. She hurtles down the steps and, arms extended, launches herself toward me, striking me just below the knees. I drop my duffel and fall on a patch of long grass.

Margaret, unaware of my brush with disaster, shouts, "He's here! He's here!" I right myself to a sitting position and give my shoulders a shake. "Zachary," she shouts, "we're here! Zachary, we came all the way to California in a big blue bus!"

Flyer lopes toward me, joining the celebration, barking. Where I sit, still on the ground, he begins licking my ear. It tickles, I laugh and inhale the warm scent of his fur.

Fumio approaches. "Flyer, take it easy, boy!" Fumio extends a hand, and as he pulls me up, without thinking I pull him to my side. My cheeks warm, but I realize this was what I saw occur between SS *Contest*'s sailors who'd survived the storm at sea. Capable men hugging each other. They together had negotiated with a typhoon and come out okay. I turn and fake punch Fumio on the arm, a move he returns.

So many people, and one dog, who mean so much to me. It's almost frightening. I oddly don't feel ready for it.

I think of those who are absent, those we've lost, those I never had a chance to know.

The young doe, Feather, believed she had lost her kid. She was frantic, confused. Sorrow nearly buried her, but in time she found her kid and herself. What if it had happened differently? What if her kid had vanished forever in the storm?

My parents lost a child. I will never know the depths of their pain. How did they, especially my mother, survive that? Someday, when it's just us, at home, in the kitchen, I'll put cookies on a plate, we'll sit together at the table, and I'll ask.

AUTHOR'S NOTE

Japan's attack on the U.S. naval base at Pearl Harbor, Hawaii, on December 7, 1941, was intended to bar the United States from interfering with aggressive actions in Southeast Asia, which were prompted by Japan's need for more resources for continued fighting, such as iron and oil. The United States entered the war the next day and remained involved until the surrender of Nazi Germany and, finally, Japan.

Before writing the story of young Zachary Whitlock, I knew nothing of the firebombing of Japan or the setting ablaze of homes, schools, churches, and hospitals. Determined to force Japan's surrender, the U.S. military in March of 1945 resorted to firebombing with a relatively new substance known as napalm. Almost as incomprehensible is the fact that the attack was codenamed "Operation Meetinghouse." Meetinghouse is what members of the Quaker faith call the place of their weekly gathering for meditation and contemplation, just as others among us refer to such a place as church or temple or synagogue or mosque.

The first target was Tokyo, where small-shop manufacturers of machine parts were intermingled with family homes, homes primarily constructed of wood. Leaflets were dropped warning of the attack, but able-bodied Japanese civilians were required by their government to fight the fire. School girls were given the task of cutting firebreaks. The assault was carefully planned. Incendiaries were dropped precisely to take advantage of the direction of heavy winds, exacerbating damage and the death toll. The firebombing of Tokyo was not made known to the national media at the time, but it has been deemed the single most destructive air raid in human history. Deaths for Tokyo alone are conservatively estimated at over one hundred thousand, with injuries at a million.

Ultimately, more than sixty cities fell prey to the attacks. The most commonly cited estimate of total Japanese casualties is 333,000 killed and eight million left homeless. Mostly civilians. Firebombing was seen as a way to end the war. It did not. Escalation to nuclear weapons came next, but atomic vengeance on Hiroshima did not end the conflict, however, and

Nagasaki, too, was later decimated. Japan surrendered on September 2, 1945. World War II lasted six years and one day, exacting a heavy toll on the world.

While *Zachary: A Seagoing Cowboy* is a work of fiction, Floyd Wilfred Schmoe was a very real person who, throughout his life, prioritized the well-being of others, disregarding personal comfort and popular recognition. A builder, writer, pacifist, and a naturalist specializing in forestry and marine biology who was well ahead of his time, Floyd Schmoe worked with passionate determination, tirelessly, for the cause of social justice. His life's story is illuminated by his dedication, humility, empathy, and kindness. I am inspired by and deeply appreciative of the family of Floyd Schmoe for their gracious response to my efforts.

Founded July 14, 1944, the Heifer Project, now Heifer International, began with a shipment of seventeen cattle from Alabama to Puerto Rico. Since then, more than seven thousand men and women have tended shipments of cattle, goats, chickens, and other farm animals being transported on land, by sea, and by air to families in need. Today, animals are most often provided through channels local to the countries served.

During WWII, refrigerated ships, sometimes called "reefers," might transport troops and, upon occasion, provided passage to civilians. In 1948, the real SS *Contest* carried Floyd Schmoe and a small team of Heifer Project volunteers—Seagoing Cowboys—to Japan.

The SS *Contest* was a Type R refrigerated cargo ship built in 1945 by the Moore Dry Dock Company in Oakland, California. An R2-S-BV1 Alstede-class stores ship, its primary mission was the transportation of goods requiring temperature control. With cross-compound turbines and a single propeller, it could achieve seventeen miles per hour.

This type of ship was typically crewed by sixty-four merchant marines, their accommodations amidships. Hot and cold running water was available. The captain's quarters were located on the bridge deck, as were the wheelhouse, chartroom, and radio room.

The outreach of Heifer International is based on a set of twelve core values known as the Cornerstones for Just and Sustainable Development. One key concept is "Passing on the Gift." Each family receiving livestock or agricultural assistance from Heifer International commits to passing along to a neighbor whatever they are given—time, goats, a cow, seeds, supplies for an irrigation system. This sharing has proven to build inclusive, locally led communities. Further support is provided through training to increase the quality and quantity of the product and by facilitating connections that will increase sales and incomes for families and communities.

Currently, Heifer International works to end hunger and improve the standard of living in nineteen countries across four continents: Bangladesh, Cambodia, Ecuador, Guatemala, Haiti, Ethiopia, Honduras, India, Kenya, Malawi, Mexico, Nepal, Nigeria, Rwanda, Senegal, Tanzania, Uganda, the United States of America and Zambia.

ACKNOWLEDGMENTS

My thanks to Peter Wick, Author/Editor/Publisher, Azzurri Publishing, who, in 2023, had the vision to produce, in an updated format, *The Years of My Day: An Eighty-Year-Long Travelogue* by Floyd Schmoe (1979). The slim volume, with its epigraph, "One day is with the Lord as a thousand years, and a thousand years as one day" (II Peter 3:8), combines text, photos, and sketches by Floyd Schmoe. Mr. Wick shares that the first edition of the book is a xeroxed, hand-bound volume he found resting on a family bookshelf, the title handwritten down the spine, and "with the blessing of the Schmoe family, we (Azzurri Publishing) have made only tiny alterations." Note: Floyd Schmoe's papers and the texts of his several books are also found in the archives of the University of Washington.

Peggy Reiff Miller's assistance has been invaluable. The recognized expert on the history of the Seagoing Cowboys and the Heifer Project, a major focus of her work has been compiling the stories of volunteer drovers who cared for livestock sent by ship to aid struggling survivors of World War II. Serving as consultant on the history of the Heifer Project, today's Heifer International, she maintains files of photos and volunteers' accounts of their experiences and is the author of the children's picture book *The Seagoing Cowboy* (Brethren Press, 2016), as well as a twice monthly blog and numerous magazine articles about the Seagoing Cowboys. For more information on Peggy Reiff Miller, see her website at www.seagoingcowboys.com.

A leading expert on national defense, space, and intelligence policy, John E. Pike is the director of Global Security, a research and consultancy group he founded in December 2000. Mr. Pike is highly regarded for his skill in making complex technical concepts readily accessible. I am immensely grateful to him for giving me permission to use a passage I think of as a Shipboard Glossary in describing Zachary's introduction to the SS *Contest*, which I reproduced exactly as Mr. Pike wrote it.

American School of Correspondence was founded in 1897. I appreciate the assistance of Catherine Leato, American Schools staff member, in confirming that First Year Algebra, Advanced Algebra, and Trigonometry courses were offered in Zachary Whitlock's era. The school today continues to offer full-year programs for students in grades six through eight, and full-year and full diploma programs for students in grades nine through twelve, as well as individual courses to aid in fulfilling course requirements and for enrichment. American School also offers a broad selection of business, career, and technical courses.

Zachary's journey toward adulthood is a story close to my heart, but *Zachary: A Seagoing Cowboy* would not exist were it not for the consistent support of writing coach and developmental editor Paula Coomer, a published novelist, culinary writer and poet, who believed in its message and mission. Ms. Coomer shared generously of her expertise, often bringing to light the glimmer that gives a story added life. I am immensely grateful.

Jimmy Kamada, my husband of sixteen years, is a man of great patience who accommodates the chimera that is a writer's mind. He has my love forever.

GLOSSARY

- arigato gozaimasu—thank you very much
- dōmo arigatō—thank you very much
- furoshiki—Japanese traditional wrapping cloth used to transport or protect objects
- geta—traditional Japanese footwear; a flat, wooden footbed elevated by two or three transverse supports, held on by a fabric thong between the first two toes
- gomennasai—I apologize
- imōto—little sister
- itadakimasu—to humbly receive, as in showing gratitude for a meal
- kyabinetto—cabinet
- kiji—Japanese green pheasant, national bird of Japan
- kimono—traditional Japanese garment, wrapped-front, square sleeves and rectangular body
- kodomo—child; literally, children
- konnichiwa—a greeting meaning hello, good day, or good afternoon
- mata kite kudasai—please come again
- obāsan—grandmother
- Obāsan—referring to one's own grandmother
- oji—uncle
- Oji—referring to one's own uncle
- ojiisan—one's mother's parents, one's grandparents
- Okāsama—referring to one's own mother, formal
- onbuhimo—traditional Japanese front-of-body baby carrier, constructed of fabric
- otearai—restroom
- Otokosan—one's own father
- otōto—younger brother
- shizukani—gentle admonition to speak quietly
- shoyu—soy sauce; a liquid condiment made from fermented soybeans, distinguished by its saltiness

FOR FURTHER READING
Floyd Schmoe

In 1988, Floyd Schmoe traveled to Japan where he was honored with the Hiroshima Peace Centre's Peace Award. He used the award money to fund the Seattle Peace Park, which opened on August 6, 1990. Floyd Wilfred Schmoe died in 2001, having lived to the age of 105.

To read more about Floyd Schmoe's work in building houses for those made homeless by the bombing of Hiroshima and Nagasaki: https://www.heifer.org/blog/a-cowboys-overseas-journey-to-rebuild-japan.html

Valuable resources for further information concerning Floyd Schmoe are:

https://www.historylink.org/File/3876
https://encyclopedia.densho.org/Floyd_Schmoe/
https://www.quakersintheworld.org/quakers-in-action/245/Floyd-Schmoe

Floyd Schmoe caring for goats aboard the SS *Contest* on his way to Japan in July 1948. *Photo courtesy of Judy Randolph, granddaughter of Floyd Schmoe.*

Floyd Schmoe (1895-2001)
(Courtesy Hiroshima Peace Memorial Museum

THE SS *CONTEST*

Information on the SS *Contest* is limited. The ship and basic statistics are listed in registries, but photographs are not found. The USS *KIDD* and the USS *SLATER*, although ships of war, are of similar size and construction, and can be studied in detail here:

USS *Kidd* https://www.usskidd.com/explore-the-kidd/
USS *Slater* https://ussslater.org/online-tour

ABOUT THE AUTHOR

Shirley Miller Kamada is a former teacher, education director, and bookstore owner. Her novel *No Quiet Water* was a finalist for the National Indie Excellence awards and the Maxy Award. She lives in Moses Lake, Washington, with her husband Jimmy and two small, adopted dogs named Priscilla and Phoenix. Learn more at shirleymillerkamada.com.

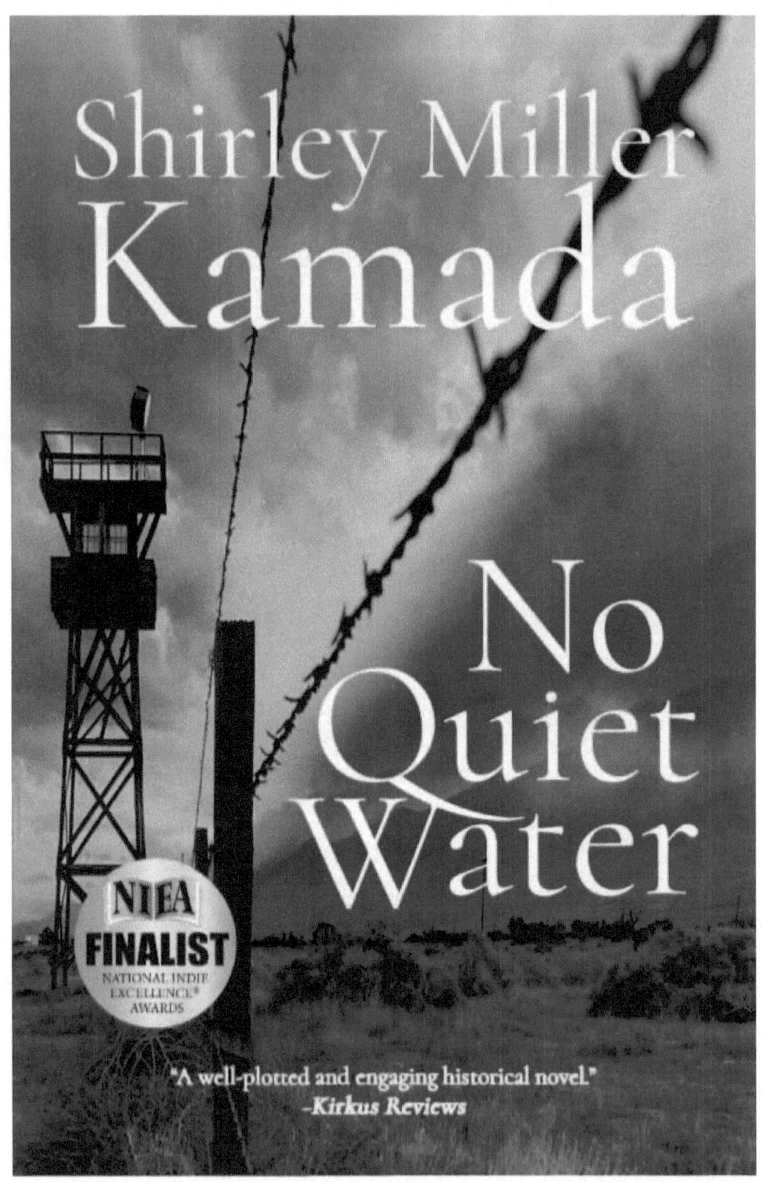
Shirley Miller
Kamada

No
Quiet
Water

NIEA
FINALIST
NATIONAL INDIE
EXCELLENCE®
AWARDS

"A well-plotted and engaging historical novel."
-Kirkus Reviews

NOTE FROM SHIRLEY MILLER KAMADA

Word-of-mouth is crucial for any author to succeed. If you enjoyed *Zachary: A Seagoing Cowboy*, please leave a review online—anywhere you are able. Even if it's just a sentence or two. It would make all the difference and would be very much appreciated.

Thanks!
Shirley Miller Kamada

We hope you enjoyed reading this title from:

www.blackrosewriting.com

Subscribe to our mailing list – *The Rosevine* – and receive **FREE** books, daily deals, and stay current with news about upcoming releases and our hottest authors.
Scan the QR code below to sign up.

Already a subscriber? Please accept a sincere thank you for being a fan of Black Rose Writing authors.

View other Black Rose Writing titles at www.blackrosewriting.com/books and use promo code **PRINT** to receive a **20% discount** when purchasing.